# THE CUTTING OF MARY PARK
and Other Devonshire Tales

Also by Ted Sherrell:

*Kingdom of Cain*
*The Lonely and the Lost*
*Milltown*
*A Bitter Wind from off the Moor*
*Nor the Years Condemn*
*Point of Order, Mr Chairman*
*And the Days Grow Short*
*Fire and the Phoenix*

# The Cutting of Mary Park

### and Other Devonshire Tales

## Ted Sherrell

**UNITED WRITERS**
Cornwall

UNITED WRITERS PUBLICATIONS LTD
Ailsa, Castle Gate, Penzance, Cornwall.

British Library Cataloguing in Publication Data:
A catalogue record for this book is
available from the British Library.

ISBN 9781852001285

Printed in Great Britain by
United Writers Publications Ltd
Cornwall.

To my wonderful wife Ann
and a family to be proud of.

# Contents

# I

# The Cutting of Mary Park

"Tell you what, boy – if this is global warming then you can keep it; let's get back to a good old fashioned cold, wet British summer." George Collins, stopped talking, and started quaffing the foaming pint of bitter which Stan Lawrence, landlord of the Shepherd's Crook, had placed before him. His fellow farmer, Harry Milton, returned a half emptied glass to the bar and nodded his agreement.

"Hot as the hods of hell it is; and it has been for months, that's the trouble. Hotter and dryer than '76 – and that's saying something."

"Too damned right," agreed his companion between gulps of the so welcome – and delightfully cool – pint of beer. "Mind you," he added, "that's over thirty years ago now – we were just lads then; able to stand it in a way you can't when you get past fifty."

"True enough," retorted Milton, nodding slowly. "You can stand things a lot better when you're young – especially extreme weather of any kind. But they're saying now, officially, that it's both hotter on average than 1976, and that there's been even less rain this year than there was then. In fact, they were saying on the BBC News the other night that it's unlikely there's ever been a spell of weather in this country as hot and dry as this one in the last four or five hundred years. Half a millennium – and there's never been anything like it before. Concentrates the mind that does, George – and with a vengeance."

"Nonsense – rubbish," came a rather querulous voice from the rear of the bar, spoken in a good, traditional Devon accent. "I'll grant you this is worse than '76, bad though that was, but it's not as bad as 1937. That's the worst year I've ever known – and I've known a few, being ninety-one years of age." The words were spoken with an air of certainty and authority, and came from the lips of the only other occupant of the bar this early Thursday evening, Tom Wilkins.

The eyes of the other three were directed in the old chap's direction. "Tom, you've been telling that old tale for years now, about 1937. According to you it was hotter and dryer than Egypt – and I don't doubt it was pretty fierce," replied Harry. "My father always talked about the summer of '37 and said it was bad. In fact, he always said it was much like '76 – although he reckoned '76 was worse in that it went on longer. Spring and summer that was, '76; in fact a warm spring with little rainfall followed a dry winter, and all this was followed by a summer – right through until early September – of baking temperatures and virtually no rainfall. So although he would have agreed that '37 was bad, he considered 1976 to be worse. But having said all that, the figures say that this year is probably the driest, hottest ever – as I said just now."

"Rubbish," insisted the old man, " 'T'was worse in '37. I've lived in this parish all my life and worked the land for most of it and I've known nothing like that; the Tamar was a quarter of normal, and the Tavy was like a stream."

"You're not still on about 1937, Tom?" came a raucous voice from seemingly just outside the pub, to be followed by a chuckle. Heads turned toward the open door just in time to see the corpulent figure of Arnold Sleeman framed in it. "You've been telling that tale ever since I can remember; I reckon I still had my milk teeth when I first heard you going on about it." Again he laughed, and went up to the bar to join the brace of fellow farmers.

"Usual, Stan, please," he replied. "And whatever everybody else is having – including yourself, of course." No sooner had the words left his mouth, than Tom belied his octogenarian years by downing the remains of his pint with all the speed of a young binge drinker. "Thank you, Arnold," said the old fellow, shuffling deftly up to the bar. "Scrumpy for me."

Stan Lawrence was one of the fast dwindling body of Devonshire publicans who still stocked rough cider – 'scrumpy'. Not that there was much demand for it these days, modern cider drinkers preferring the far more refined and infinitely less potent twenty-first century drink which was akin to a sparkling apple wine and bore little resemblance to the rather muddy looking, powerful, brew that was scrumpy. Old Tom though, and half of the other regulars at the pub, invariably elderly men, who were regular scrumpy drinkers, all complained that the modern brew was not in the same league as that which they had known as young men; which was undoubtedly true, as Stan Lawrence knew very well. As he had explained to Tom and most of the other regular drinkers on many occasions over recent years, there was no way modern day health inspectors and environmental officers were going to allow the 'witches brew', that was the traditional scrumpy of their younger years, to be sold to the general public. "It would just about kill the youngsters today – and those that survived would be looking for a punch up even more than they are at present."

As it was, the ageing landlord didn't sell a great deal of the pungent and still very potent brew, and he had little doubt that when he retired – which would be within the next five years at the most – the new publican would stop stocking it.

Arnold raised his glass, muttered "Cheers" and downed half of it in one gargantuan gulp. "Nectar," he said. "Sort of weather you can drink a pub dry. Not that I can afford to, mind you; if this weather goes on much longer, I'll scarce be able to afford a single pint. And it's going to go on as far as I can see – don't think there's any talk of any change in the weather. Mind you, I have to admit that I've not listened to a forecast for a week or more. What's the point – I mean it must be as easy to give our weather forecast these days as it is in Saudi Arabia. Dry and hot – the only variation being when the hot weather gets even hotter."

"I'm much the same," agreed George Collins. "I've not listened to radio forecasts – or even TV ones for that matter – for some time. The trouble is they always seem to start off with Scotland and by the time they reach Devon and Cornwall my attention has long gone. The number of times I've listened to, or watched the forecast and then when Jill's asked me what it is, I don't know – daft isn't it? What I do these days is to flip it up on the text – that way you can read it in your own time, and choose your own region first. In normal times I do anyway. I've not even done this in the past couple of weeks – these are not normal times are they? I find it all a bit depressing – the same old tale day in, day out."

Sleeman nodded, the expression on his face now far more serious. "Yes –it's all a bit depressing and no mistake. I know one thing – if it doesn't change soon and we get rain, and a lot of rain as well, then I'll be done for."

The landlord looked up from drying a few glasses. "What do you mean – done for, Arnold? That's a bit dramatic, isn't it?"

"No boy, it isn't. I mean, in the last dozen to fifteen years, I've known disaster after disaster; we all have. BSE, crippling EC regulations and red tape, ever lowering returns, the foot and mouth – then even worse returns. Yet we've kept going, all of us; but there'll be no way round this, not if it doesn't rain soon – and I mean very soon. I've scarce got a blade of grass on the farm, and I'm forced to feed the stock with the hay I've got left from last year; I've already used up the little I made this summer. Not surprisingly, the cows are scarce producing enough milk to look after our morning cornflakes – so there's virtually no income in that direction. In fact, there's no real income in any direction at present. And the stock – sheep as well – are going back full gallop. I'm ashamed to see them; all the years I've been farming – and my father before me – it's the first time I've ever had bullocks running on any land of mine where you could see their ribs. With just about all of mine now, you can count every rib they've got – I feel ashamed."

"None of your fault, Arnold – mine's much the same," comforted George Collins.

"Granted – but I still feel ashamed. Like you George – and you Harry – farming's always been more to me than just making a living; it's been about pride – about a job well done. After all, that's why we all continue to do it – why none of us have walked away from it in recent times, even though things have been so bad; even though none of us have anybody to take over from us; you've got no kids, George, whilst my two boys turned their backs on it long ago and have got decent well paid jobs. And you, Harry, your lad Martin has gone into contracting, whilst your maid has gone to Australia – and not to farm either. No, we've kept going through a combination of cussedness and a lingering affection for a way of life that's been in our families for generations. It'll all end though, and soon, if it doesn't rain in the very near future – as far as I'm concerned, anyway."

"End – what do you mean, end?" The question from the lips of Stan Lawrence was sharp, urgent.

"Well the end of our stock – the end of us farming, Angie and me. We're already out of water – totally. We're not on mains, and we've always relied on a well close to our house for ourselves, and a brook down in the valley for the stock. Over the years, whilst the pumps have packed up from time to time, this year, for the first time ever, it's the supplies that have packed up. The pumps are both working all right, but there's nothing there for them to pump up. It's never happened before – not in living memory anyway. Not even in 1937, or so I'm told," he said, quite loudly, his eyes momentarily on Tom Wilkins sitting in his usual place near the fireplace at the back of the bar, supping his pint. The old man appeared not to hear him, his mind seemingly elsewhere. Arnold smiled, a little wearily, and looked back towards Stan Lawrence on the other side of the bar. "The supply down in the valley packed up nearly three weeks back, whilst the well went dry just a couple of days ago. At present I'm spending half of every day going around to Dick Davey's place with the old pick up, half a dozen old churns aboard that I've found about the place, and bringing them back full of water. Then I tip them in the troughs; the stock – especially the cows – come round, put their snouts in it, and seemingly within seconds, the bloody trough's

13

empty. So it's back to Dick's place again with the churns – I did it nine times yesterday. Now, of course, we've got to have one for our own use as well. Good water, mind you, at Dick's. He's got a bore hole which must go down to the centre of the earth 'cause there never seems to be any decrease in the flow. Damned good of him, of course – but then, that's the sort of chap he is. When the hay's gone though – it's a very different story then. I don't have to pay for the water, but hay and forage will be a very different tale. I've not even bothered to ask what the merchants are demanding for it at the moment; it's never cheap, but in times like these – well, I reckon it's as dear as saffron."

"Saffron would be cheaper," rasped Harry Milton with a sad shake of his head, obviously having enquired as to the price of it.

Arnold nodded. "Inevitable, isn't it. One thing's for sure, I'll be buying none of it. We're in deep enough at the bank as it is – start buying hay and suchlike, and it's the bankruptcy court for us. No, when the fodder runs out – and it's not much more than a week away – then it's the slaughter house for our stock; cows, bullocks, calves, sheep, everything except the dog and the cats. Heartbreaking – but sadly it'll be the easiest of decisions, simply because there is no other one possible." He shook his head – and closed his eyes; truly a man defeated.

The landlord of the Shepherd's Crook looked stunned. "Slaughter house?" he croaked. "You mean you'll kill them all – why, why for God's sake? If you can't keep them, then sell them – sell them; don't kill them."

"Arnold'll have no option – nor shall I, or Harry," responded George. "I've probably a bit longer and Harry as well, I suspect, but it's early August now and if it hasn't rained by the end of the month, then my stock, my pride and joy if I'm honest, will be in lorries on the way to the slaughter house as well. There's no way round it."

Once again Stan Lawrence was about to open his mouth in a plea to sell rather than kill, only to have the cry stilled in his throat by George Collins timely intervention.

"We can't sell the beasts, Stan – there's no market. At the moment, we'd not be able to give them away – and I mean that literally. And I don't mean just around here; I mean right throughout the country – the British Isles, from Land's End to John O'Groats. That is possibly the unique aspect of this drought – everywhere, England, Scotland, Wales, Ireland have been hit by it. There's not a decent field of grain throughout the land. No food for them – nothing, nowhere. They've already started slaughtering in parts of the Midlands and East Anglia. Horrific it is. But also inevitable – unless it rains. And we'll get nothing for the animals – in fact, it'll cost us by the time we pay for transport and the slaughterer's costs."

"But the government'll compensate you, surely?" pleaded the landlord. "I mean, it'll lead to thousands of farms throughout the country going out of business – going bankrupt in fact."

"That it will," nodded Arnold, "but in fairness to the government – and it's rare I'm ever fair to this lot – but in fairness to them, there's no way they can pay compensation; that would bankrupt the country. After all, you're not thinking of slaughter on the scale of the foot and mouth epidemic of 2001 – massive though that was. No, you're talking here now of countless millions of animals being put down, everywhere – every square mile of this country, rural and urban alike is affected by this wicked drought, and this infernal heat. The government could scarce afford to reimburse the cost of transporting the stock to the slaughter houses, let alone anything else. No, there'll be no compensation, Stan – just endless fields empty of stock, and looking very, very, brown."

The landlord, deeply shocked to hear of the probable fate of the livestock of the nation, was about to pursue the subject once more, but was diverted – to the secret relief of the farmers who did not want to talk any more about the probable destruction of their stock.

Although like most farmers they were not remotely sentimental, they saw the animals which trod their fields as the focal point of their way of life, as well as the core of their making a living. None of them had the mental strength to think what their lives would be like, what future they had, if this drought caused the slaying of the treasured beasts.

Stan Lawrence was forced to leave the subject, though, and the three solemn farmers, to serve a young couple who, a couple of minutes earlier, had passed through the bar to the shady, very pleasant beer garden at the back, set quite high up overlooking the Tamar Valley. They had returned inside to order a couple of drinks and a meal from the small but good value menu chalked up on the board at the far end of the bar. Stan would take their order, then pass it through to his wife Sally – an excellent cook. The pub did reasonably well through the week, regarding its meals side, and extremely well at weekends, its good, tasty food, and very large portions, encouraging a sizeable number of regular customers.

The landlord returned to his regulars just as George was explaining that whilst his own deep borehole was still producing just enough to keep his stock going, he felt that it was not far from going dry. "Still," he said wearily, "we'll be no worse off than most of the country. They were saying on TV just a couple of nights back, that the government have sent instructions to all the water authorities and local councils throughout the land about how to handle things if everywhere – including the cities, of course – have to go on stand pipes. When you think of it, it'll be hellish. Think of hospitals and places like that – schools, as well, of course. Chaos it'll be. In fact, there could well be civil disorder. A lot of folk are poor at dealing with minor inconveniences, so God knows how they'll react to having no water in their taps. No, with all they've got on their plate already – and with the situation if stand pipes come – they'll not be worrying too much about all the livestock being put down. Inevitable, I'm afraid." The farmer glanced up at the returned landlord. "Got some eating customers then Stan," he stated. "It's only half past six – you don't usually get anybody in until later do you?"

"No – usually after seven; in fact, usually after half past seven, especially week days. But they're on holiday hereabouts, so they've not had to get home from work like so many customers. One good thing is that I should be able to sell them a bottle or two of wine, or a few pints – for they'll surely have a thirst on them after they've eaten, seeing what they've ordered. He wants a curry and she's having a chilli – on a hot night like this! And you know Sally's curries."

They did indeed; for the landlady's curries were famed throughout West Devon. In fact, it was claimed that nobody could be so cold even on the bitterest day in winter, that they could not be warmed by one of her curries. The farmers looked quite stunned. "He doesn't know what he's taken on," laughed Harry. "There's many an Indian who'd not be able to handle one of Sally's curries."

"Well they'll be drinking a fair bit, as I said just now."

"As long as it's not water," retorted Arnold Sleeman. "We can't spare any of that – for certain." His all too true words brought silence and a pall to the gathering. The farming trio sat at the bar gazing ahead somewhat morosely, while Stan Lawrence prepared the drinks which the young couple had ordered, and then proceeded to take them, along with cutlery for their meal, through the back door of the capacious bar into the beer garden beyond.

Just as he was returning through the door, a cry rent the almost oppressive silence – one which would have almost awoken the dead. It certainly startled the landlord and other customers alike.

"Hells bells, Tom, what's that about?" croaked Lawrence, genuinely alarmed. "You've not said a word in ten minutes, then you yell like a lunatic. What's the matter?"

"Mary Park, that's what's the matter. The way to break this drought, that's what's the matter. The salvation of this parish – who knows, perhaps even the entire country, that's what's the matter."

Nobody had ever seen the old fellow as animated as he was at that moment; to be honest, however, as George Collins remarked to somebody a few days later, nobody to his knowledge had ever seen Tom Wilkins animated at all.

"Anyway, who's Mary Park?" enquired Harry Milton. "There's a lot of new folk in the village these days, so she must be one of these. I'd know her for sure if she'd been here very long. I know most of the people that have been in the village for some time."

"Most of the folk I know in the village these days are up in the churchyard," retorted Arnold, a touch acidly. "I still go up now and again and put a few flowers on mother and father's grave, and as I walk past the headstones and read the names, I know just about all of them – frightening it is."

Tom was so anxious to tell as to who Mary Park was, that he had choked on his scrumpy and went into a long, slightly alarming coughing fit.

Knowing that an old fellow of ninety-one pegging out in his pub would not be an ideal way to end a day, Stan quickly drew off a glass of water from the tap, and took it round to his elderly customer, still coughing and wheezing a little, although much improved from what he was.

Tom took the glass and gulped down virtually half its contents with the speed of a binge drinker.

"Must be just about the first time Tom's drunk water in his life," muttered George with a light smile playing around his lips.

With four sets of eyes riveted to him, Tom eventually ceased coughing, regained his composure, then began to explain his enigmatic outburst. "Mary Park's not a woman," he rasped, "it's a field. You chaps must know that?" he snorted, viewing the trio of farmers. "After all, you've lived in the parish all your lives. You surely must know Mary Park – especially you, Harry, it's on Oaklands Rise, the next farm to you."

The light of recognition flooded Milton's face. "Yes, 'course, 'course, Tom. Sorry I've been so thick; it's this blasted heat, I fancy – addled my brains. Good field for mushrooms as I recall. Not that there'll be many mushrooms about unless it rains. If it did, though – poured that is – then the ground would be white with them; heat and then rain, that's mushroom weather."

"I'm not fussed about the mushrooms – although I'm partial to them with a fried breakfast. No, what I'm saying is that if Mary Park is cut to hay, then it'll break the drought; you'll have all the rain you need – and possibly a lot more besides."

"Still don't follow you, Tom," interrupted Arnold. "What's rain got to do with cutting the grass in Mary Park – that's if there is any grass there; if it's like every other field in the parish, there'll be precious little."

"It don't matter in the slightest how much or how little grass there is," persisted the old fellow. "It's the cutting of whatever is there that's the crucial thing. If you put a grass cutter to Mary Park it'll rain – and within a couple of days as well, perhaps even quicker. The number of times that's happened over the years; in fact I know several of the old farmers who'd never cut their own grass when Mary Park was cut. They knew it would bring rain."

"Always?" Stan Lawrence's voice was sharp, urgent. In the back of his mind a voice was telling him that this ancient man was talking absolute nonsense, yet the situation for these good men who had frequented his pub throughout the fifteen years he had owned the Shepherd's Crook – and whom he saw as friends as well as good customers – was so bleak, that even though the tale sounded like a load of hogwash, anything, no matter how daft, was worth pursuing if it meant that this vicious drought could be broken.

The old man considered the abrupt question, then backed off, slightly, from giving a totally affirmative answer. "Well, I don't ever recall a time when it didn't work," responded Stan truthfully. For he didn't, but he was aware that an old memory like his could be prone to playing the odd trick. "It'll work – I know it'll work. I've never been more convinced of anything in my life. You fellows want to get around to Oaklands Rise, see Arthur Symons, and tell him he's got to cut that field of hay. That'll bring rain, just you see if it doesn't. Go now – go around and have a word with Arthur. He'll listen to you – good man, Arthur, one of the old school."

"Well, one thing's for certain," retorted George Collins, "we'll have to take a shovel with us if we want to get hold of Arthur. He was planted in the churchyard about five, six years back."

Tom Wilkins slapped his forehead in frustration. " 'Course – yes, you're right. I'd forgotten that; I shouldn't have, mind you – I remember going to the funeral. Well, whatever, what you need to do – and right away – is to go around to Oaklands Rise and have a chat with the owner, whoever that is; I should know that – who the owner is. I usually know things like that."

Indeed, the old fellow generally did know things like that – the comings and goings in the parish, certainly on the long established farms, had long been of immense interest to him. In fact, one of his favourite pastimes was to bemoan the fact that a majority of the farms, agricultural and horticultural holdings in the parish were in the hands of newcomers, most of whom had not bought the places to make a living from the land. In most instances, the often large, well built farmhouses were the attraction, the land being let – or sometimes sold – to other farmers, or big landowners (many of them business syndicates and companies). Occasionally, on the small holdings, the land was used in a somewhat haphazard way, by the owners to indulge a hobby, or augment income – not to actually try to make a living from. In fairness, the days had long gone when a living was to be made from the land, unless that being farmed was at least 100 acres in size – in fact, far more if any half decent income was to be gained.

"Hang on," said Wilkins. "Isn't it somebody called Smith or Jones, something like that; sort of surname that's quite common, sort of business."

"It used to be a fellow called Dougie Smith," interjected a voice from the end of the bar, "but he left about eight or nine months ago. There's a family there now by the name of Mason – man, woman and a couple of kids; girls."

All eyes suddenly switched to the source of the voice – Jimmy Parker, one of the local postmen.

"Excuse me interrupting," continued Parker, "but I overheard what you were talking about just as I came into the bar. Yes, they moved in there just after the Smiths moved out – they went back to the London area, I think. Unusual in itself, that is – it's generally the other way round these days, all these blasted people coming in and forcing up house prices well beyond anything local folk can afford."

There were grunts, murmurings and noddings of agreement over what the postman had said.

"I'm not sure where the Masons have come from, but I don't think it's the London area; it could be the Midlands though. They get several letters with a Birmingham postmark sent to them. They both work, I think – although I don't know what they do.

Most of the land they let out to that new fellow over at Barton Park – Browning he's called. Another newcomer, of course – been in the Parish for less than a couple of years, don't know where he came from."

"Nor I," said Arnold Sleeman, "but at least he's a serious farmer – and quite a good one from what I've heard and seen."

The postman nodded. "Yes – reckon you're right, Arnold," he agreed, taking the pint proffered him by Stan Lawrence, which was pulled without any instruction, Parker being another regular. The postman raised his pint in the direction of Sleeman who had put down a fiver to cover the drink, feeling it was the least he could do with Parker providing so much useful information.

"Cheers, Arnold – gents." The pint was lifted into the air, then put to rest upon the postman's lips until a goodly amount of it had been consumed. He put it down onto the bar, wiped his lips with the back of his hand, and continued the giving of information regarding Oaklands Rise. "They've still got a couple of fields, mind you, 'cause they keep a couple of horses – for the girls, I think. A small paddock in front of the house, and that big four or five acre field next to it."

"Mary Park," Tom retorted, "that's Mary Park – still part of Oaklands Rise. It's got to be cut to hay – that'll break this drought without a shadow of doubt. You want to get round there right away you chaps – this very evening – and persuade him to cut it."

"Perhaps it's already been cut," argued Harry, though without any great conviction in his voice.

" 'Course it's not," replied the old fellow, a little tersely. "If it had been cut it would have rained by now."

The logic was a touch lopsided, but devastating nonetheless – and the group fell silent.

The silence was broken by Jimmy Parker who opined, "I can't be certain, but I don't think it's been cut. I go there most days – they have quite a bit of mail – but I don't recall seeing any grass lying there. Mind you, there's not much grass lying anywhere in the parish where they have cut it. Same with corn; hardly any yield and even less straw."

"Too true," agreed Arnold. "There's some fields in the parish –

21

spring sown mainly – where the stalk is so short they can't get the combine's blade low enough to cut it. They've just got to treat it like fodder for the stock and turn cows and bullocks in to graze. It keeps the stock going in the short term, of course, but it means that in reality there won't really be a corn harvest for many folk; anybody in deep at the banks at present, it could well push them into the bankruptcy court."

There were general mutterings of agreement for a few seconds, but this was brought to an abrupt halt by an impatient bellow from Tom Wilkins.

"It don't matter about cutting corn – cutting Mary Park is what you should be concentrating on," rasped he. "It'll end this drought – mark my words." A sudden expression of inspiration flitted across his lined, weather-hardened face. "It broke the 1937 drought," cried he, triumphantly. "I remember it well. Cyril Symons – Arthur's father – farmed it then. Several farmers went round to see him, as I recall, and begged him to cut it, but he didn't want to 'cause rough though it was, it was the only field on the farm that had any grass in it. So he refused to do it; but then they got the vicar to go round and he was able to talk him into it; Reverend Billings – master preacher. I don't know what he said, but that very same day he got out his grass cutter, hitched a team of 'orses up to it, and cut it. And he never saved one blade of it, 'cause in less than two days it had rained. Early September, that was – far too late to cut grass to hay in any normal times. Whatever, he cut it and it scarce stopped raining from then till Christmas. I remember it like yesterday."

Dubious glances were cast the way of the old chap by his fellow drinkers, none of them convinced that the memories from virtually seventy years earlier of a very elderly gentleman could be relied upon. There was, though, no denying that Tom had spoken with both passion and utter conviction.

"And whilst that's the main time it happened, it's worked many other times as well – 1976 being a good example."

"I don't recall it working in '76," replied George Collins, "and I remember that year all too well even though it was more than thirty years back. No, I don't recall anything like that Tom."

"That's 'cause you weren't looking for it, boy," replied Wilkins with easy logic. "It just rained and you thought it was the natural way of things, when all along it was down to Mary Park being cut."

Harry Milton looked somewhat bemused, then shrugged his shoulders. "I'm not convinced about this at all – old wives' tale Tom, that's what it is. It could be that a time or two over the years – over the decades – it has rained after the grass has been cut on Mary Park, coincidentally, then somebody claimed that it was its cutting that brought the rain. There's nothing easier than starting superstitions such as that. No, I don't buy it, boy – although I'd be delighted if such a thing was true. Sorry, Tom – but I fancy it's a load of old nonsense."

Tom's face turned a bright shade of purple – clearly he was about to erupt; but before he could, George interjected. "Well it's a bit of a tall tale, true, but it could be right – who knows. I've certainly heard this before, about cutting Mary Park – but I've not the faintest idea whether there's any truth in it or not. Some of these old superstitions can be based on some solid foundation, I have to say." He shrugged his shoulders. "I don't know what to believe, to tell you the truth."

"Stuff and nonsense," snorted Arnold Sleeman. "I don't believe a word of it – although I respect what you're saying Tom, don't get me wrong. I've known you long enough to realise you'd only say what you believed." He did not wish to offend the old chap – so said the words in as soothing a way as possible.

"You don't offend me, Arnold," came the retort. "But you do try my patience; I'm suggesting to you – all of you – a way to end this dreadful drought, one that by your own admission could put you all out of business in the next few weeks, perhaps even the next fortnight, and you take no notice of me. Why not? Go round to this young fellow at Oaklands Rise and get him to cut Mary Park. If the superstition is right, then it'll rain – and you'll all be saved. If it's not, then the drought'll carry on – clearly. But at least you'll know you've tried. Good God, what have you got to lose? Do it – do it now, before it's too late."

For several seconds silence reigned in the bar. It was broken by

George Collins. "You know, Tom, you can be surprisingly persuasive at times." He shook his head. "I don't believe it – not a word of it, if I'm honest. Yet I'm a countryman born and bred, and I do know that things happen – always have – that bear no logic. This could be such a thing. You're right when you say we've nothing to lose – nothing at all. I have to say that I'm coming round to the idea that perhaps we should go around to Oaklands Rise and get this fellow Mason to cut Mary Park."

Harry Milton shook his head, somewhat sadly. "I don't think I can go along with this. I'd stand in front of this fellow feeling an absolute idiot. I'd not know where to look."

"Me likewise," nodded Arnold Sleeman. "My God, he would stand there thinking he was in the company of maniacs. Some of these folk from up the line think themselves superior to us as it is. I shudder to think what his reaction would be to all this."

George smiled, somewhat wearily. "You could well be right, Arnold – and you Harry. Yet, I've got to the stage when I'm that desperate, I'm willing to try anything – as long as it's legal and moral, as the saying goes."

"Well said, George," enthused Tom. "That's the only way to look at it. It's worked in the past, that I do know – almost miraculously, but worked nonetheless. You've got to go and see him – all of you. It'll be the best day's work you've done in many a year. Even if you've got to pay him compensation, it'll be worth it."

"Compensation?" Arnold almost choked on his beer. "What do you mean compensation – I'll pay no compensation to anybody. It's a daft enough idea to start with, without money changing hands. What made you think of that, Tom?"

"Well, old Cyril Symons asked for payment. He wouldn't cut a blade of the grass until the fellows who went to see him agreed on some compensation," said the old man.

"They paid money to get him to put a blade to his own grass?" Arnold Sleeman was so incredulous, his voice had the sound of strangulation. "I've never heard anything so totally daft in all of my life. They had to be mazed as sheep to agree to something like that."

24

"They were desperate, Arnold," he retorted. "They had their backs to the wall just like you fellows have now – willing to try anything. And it made sense for old Cyril to ask for some payment. That was the only grass he had on Oaklands Rise – the only grass he had to keep his stock going just a bit longer. If he'd cut it, and no rain had come, all he'd have had was a poor field of hay. And they understood that – so they agreed to pay him; I don't know how much it was, but for sure it was money few of them could afford. Those were the 'thirties remember – far far harder times than today. But as things turned out, it was the best money they ever spent."

"And you're sure it worked, Tom – you're sure it rained soon after?" George Collins was looking deep into the old fellow's eyes, it was a question as serious as any he had ever asked.

"Certain, boy. It rained – poured, in fact – within a couple of weeks. And went on right through the autumn. In fact, I fancy that within a few days of the rain coming, there was some flooding in the lower part of the parish."

Stan Lawrence put down a glass he was polishing, and spoke for the first time in several minutes. "It seems to me you chaps have no real option. You've got to go along to Oaklands Rise and get this new chap there to cut Mary Park. It may not work, of course, but these are desperate times for you all – so you've got to take desperate measures."

"He'll laugh in our faces, Stan," snorted Arnold. "He's not a local man so, like so many who come to this area these days, he'll no doubt think we're a bunch of straw chewing yokels with the IQ of goats. He'll have a whale of a time telling his family and friends about it – and we'll never be able to lift our heads again, not in this parish anyhow."

"Sadly, I think you're probably right, Arnold," agreed Harry. "He probably will laugh at us – behind our backs, at least. Yet what Stan says is right enough – these are desperate times, the most desperate any of us have ever known. If it doesn't rain soon – very soon – we'll all be ruined; none of us are getting any younger, so it'll mean we'll face a pretty barren old age – our wives as well. It all sounds daft, and probably is daft – but if by

25

some amazing chance it were to work, then feeling like a fool would be a very, very cheap price to pay for having our businesses, and our way of life saved."

George Collins nodded in agreement. "Like you, Harry, I think this is the old wives' tale to end them all. But I'll try anything to end this drought, and whilst I don't think that this will do it, I'll give it a go; and if I look like a fool, then so be it. I'll certainly feel like one. But nothing ventured, nothing gained. It's a bit late to go around there this evening, but perhaps we could meet here tomorrow evening – after tea, say – and go out there and have a chat with this fellow Mason."

"Agreed, boy," replied Harry Milton, a brisk, determined tenor to his voice. "I reckon we'll all feel a bit daft going out to see this chap, a stranger to this area – in fact, a stranger to the West Country as a whole – and telling him such a ridiculous yarn based on a totally silly superstition, but if it would make it rain, then I'd go around there and chant eeny, meeny, miney, mo, standing on my head. Are you with us, Arnold?"

Sleeman emptied his glass and dropped it back onto the bar, ready to take his leave. "Do you know," he replied, "I've been coming into this pub so long it doesn't bear thinking about; yet I can not ever remember being involved in such a daft conversation as we've had about Mary Park at any time in my entire life – and I've never heard a dafter suggestion than that we go out there tomorrow and tell this tale in seriousness, to some cynical stranger. Yet I will go with you; we've lived our entire lives in this parish, the three of us. We went to school together, went out as young men together – in fact, I suppose we went courting together, although we were all picked off by the women in our lives at different times," he laughed. "And certainly for a very long time we've all drunk together in this pub – since long before old Stan here was landlord, and that in itself, is a fair time. So I reckon we are old, good and very long standing friends. So, out of loyalty, I'll shelve my dignity and scepticism and I will come with you tomorrow night – and may the Lord have mercy on all our souls; and our reputations."

"That settles it then. We'll meet here tomorrow night at, say, seven o'clock. Then we'll go out to Oaklands Rise and see if we can make it rain. And I hope I feel a little less of a fool than I do now." George Collins had spoken briskly, and practically; the decision had been made – and the following night a serious request was to be made to what would be, no doubt, an astonished stranger, that he cut what little grass was in the larger of his two fields in order that a debilitating, record breaking, soul destroying drought be broken.

Another blistering day preceded the meeting of the three farmers in the bar of the Shepherd's Crook. The trio arrived almost at the same time – just before seven o'clock. They eyed each other somewhat sheepishly, before Arnold muttered, "Well, I don't know about you blokes, but I'm going to have a Scotch before I go; I need a bit of 'Dutch' courage for this one – I'm going to feel a bloody fool even though I shan't be doing the talking."

Harry Milton's normal lugubrious expression became a little animated. "I hadn't thought about that – who is going to do the talking? A good point, that is, certainly it's one we should sort out here and now. We just need one to speak for all of us. With that in mind, I nominate you, George. After all, whilst you've not been enthusiastic about pursuing this business, you've been far less sceptical than Arnold and myself; certainly you'll be better at telling a more convincing tale than we will."

Collins shrugged his shoulders. "Fair enough – I don't mind doing it, though I'm not looking forward to it. One thing I do feel though is that we shouldn't have anything to drink; so I reckon your Scotch ought to wait 'til we've been there. After all, Arnold, if any of us go out there stinking of whisky, beer, anything alcoholic, he'll probably think we're drunk with our request sounding like the ramblings of folk the worse for liquor. You see what I mean?"

Arnold Sleeman nodded his agreement: "Yes, fair comment, George. We'll keep the drinking 'til afterwards; we'll have earned a few by then – you especially as you're doing the talking."

In less than fifteen minutes, the three farmers were sitting in

27

the quite expensively furnished lounge at Oaklands Rise. Obviously no shortage of money in the Mason family surmised the trio as they sat in easy chairs about the large room. Their host, a tall, well built fellow of some forty years – most courteous and welcoming to his unexpected guests – looked around at his visitors. "Can I offer you a drink gentlemen – alcoholic, or otherwise? I've got a very pleasant single malt for anybody who enjoys their Scotch."

Arnold brightened up right away; it was one thing to arrive exuding breath which carried nothing more offensive than a slight whiff of spring onions from the salad he had consumed an hour earlier, but it could be no 'hanging offense' to rinse out the mouth with the decent whisky that was being offered by their host. "Thank you, Mr Mason – that'll be great," he enthused.

Their host gazed at the other two. "Gentlemen?"

"I'll have a Scotch as well, thank you," nodded Harry.

"I'm not a whisky man, to be honest, Mr Mason," said George, "but a nice glass of beer – or lager – would go down well thank you."

Mason turned to go. "I'll only be a couple of minutes; and please call me Phil."

He was a touch more than two minutes, although not a lot, returning with a tray upon which there were three whiskies and a pint glass of lager. Having handed them around, he took his own glass, seated himself in the sole unoccupied chair, and raised his glass to his guests. "Cheers, gentlemen."

Glasses were raised in response. "Cheers, Phil," they chorused and George Collins, seeing an opportunity to divert to the subject which motivated their visit, added, "and here's to the end of this wretched drought."

Phil Mason swallowed a goodly portion of the generous measure of whisky in his glass – like amounts being in the tumblers held by Arnold and Harry – then replied: "Yes, I would drink to that – and cooler weather as well. My wife and I are both what would be termed 'sun worshippers', but this has really got out of hand. We only moved into Oaklands Rise last October, as you probably know, so our first summer here has been a real

28

baptism of fire – almost literally. As I said, we both enjoy hot weather, and can handle it, but a drought such as this one is another matter. Clearly it is exceptionally serious, with the problems associated with it multiplying by the day."

"Absolutely, Mr – I mean, Phil," agreed Collins. "The reality is that they have multiplied to such an extent now, it's difficult to see any way of solving them unless it rains very, very soon, and continues to do so, on and off, for weeks, even months to come; which brings us, in effect, to the reason we've invaded your home – and taken advantage of your excellent hospitality this evening." There was nothing wrong with a bit of flattery, he mused, at a time such as this. "I've been elected by my colleagues here to do the talking, Mr Mason – as it's largely down to me that we are here taking up your valuable time. Having said that, I have to admit it's very difficult to explain exactly why we are here. In fact, I fancy that when I've told you the reason you might show us the door – even worse, you might think you're in the company of a bunch of lunatics."

Their host laughed. "I doubt that very much," said he. "But I was wondering when you came, what I could do for you, so now I really am intrigued as to the purpose of your visit – welcome though it is." Being essentially a courteous man, he felt it only right to add the last four words.

"It's about this drought, er . . . Phil," Collins continued, looking anywhere but at his host who had a rather disconcerting way of gazing at one with scarce a blinking of his eyes. What he was about to say was embarrassing enough, without being under the intense scrutiny of such a stare. "The simple fact is we've never known anything like it in this parish in our lifetime."

"That's because there's never been anything like it in this parish – or in any other parish throughout the land – for centuries. Possibly there's not been a drought as severe as this in a thousand years and more." Phil Mason spoke the words easily, but with a tone that suggested he was well aware of the accuracy of what he was saying.

"Absolutely, Phil – totally right," George agreed. "The trouble is, though, that if it doesn't break soon we'll all be ruined – the farming community, that is. There's virtually no grass left anywhere, and precious little water. If it doesn't rain, Phil, we're about a fortnight – at best – away from a mass slaughter of stock in this parish; stock which has no monetary value at all when dead, because there'll be a similar slaughter throughout large parts, if not all, the country. Millions of animals slain everywhere and no market for the meat. It doesn't bear thinking about – yet, obviously, we have to think of it."

"It really is that bad, eh?" The tone of Mason's voice was soft and sympathetic.

Arnold Sleeman nodded and spoke a terse, "Yes, that serious, I'm afraid."

"And because of the calamity we all face, Phil, we've come to see you," continued George, still not looking at him. "I doubt you are aware of it – there's no reason why you should be – but there's a superstition that's been around amongst our local community for generations. It concerns one of your fields here at Oaklands Rise."

Mason laughed. "This gets more interesting and intriguing by the minute, gents."

"Yes, well I suppose it is interesting in a way," agreed the farmer, the sweat pouring from him caused by the strain of telling this bizarre tale even more than by the warmth and humidity of the evening. "It's a bit silly as well, in all honesty – especially to somebody like yourself from outside the area. I mean – I doubt you'll have much belief in superstitions and old wives' tales."

"Oh, I don't know about that – there are few people anywhere, when push comes to shove, who have no superstition about them," he articulated. "I have a few superstitions I subscribe to – as does my wife. A goodly number when I come to think of it. No, my dear chap, it is not only rural Devonians who believe in such things. We so called sophisticated city folk also have our strange, illogical and, often, alarm causing beliefs."

Mason's confession made George Collins feel a great deal better; if this most affable man could understand the power of superstition then it made it easier for him to say what he had to.

"Well, Phil, to get to the nub of what we've come here for

tonight," he proceeded, far more briskly and confidently than before (indeed he was now able to look Mason in the face), "it is to make a very unusual request to you. As I said just now, the superstition concerns one of your two fields – the much larger one, Mary Park. Now the belief has long been, and remains strong amongst many of the older locally born folk, that dry spells, even droughts, are often – some say, always – ended when Mary Park has its grass cut."

Their host was clearly about to laugh, but, his natural courtesy stopped him doing so. Rather he chuckled, briefly, then opined, "That sounds just a little bit unlikely. In fact, to be quite frank, it sounds just a touch ridiculous."

George Collins was anxious to agree with the man – the occasion called for nothing less. "Yes, yes, it does, Phil," replied he, quickly. "We're told though – by older folk," said he a little lamely – for none of the trio sat before the newcomer in this room could have been described as being young, "that if the field is cut, then rain will come – within a day or two, at the most. Granted there's never been a drought like this before, as you were saying just now, but these folk claim that it has ended some very serious droughts in the past, 1937 and '76 being amongst them, as well as several other summers which, whilst not drought ridden, had long, hot and destructive dry spells – destructive for farming that is."

"So you want me to cut the grass in Mary Park," stated Phil Mason, coming quickly and very directly to the point of their visit.

"Well – well, yes," agreed George Collins, backed up by vigorous nodding of the heads of his two companions, all of them slightly nonplussed by their host's directness. "Yes, that's about it, Phil. It's probably all a load of old nonsense," continued the farmer a touch sheepishly, "but as I said earlier, we're in a situation so desperate that we're willing to try anything, no matter how daft it might sound."

"That's quite understandable, gentlemen. I'm fortunate, of course, in that I do not make my living from the land. If I did, then I've no doubt I'd be as desperate as you are – as the farming community throughout the land are. I just keep the two fields for my horses to graze in. My daughters love riding – like so many young girls do; and my wife saddles up occasionally. I'm not a horse man myself, conscious of the fact that – as somebody once put it so succinctly – they bite at one end and kick at the other. The small paddock has already been cut, of course – back in June. I'd hoped and expected there to be rain well before now to bring on another decent crop of grass, but a forlorn hope, sadly. As for Mary Park, there's precious little in there even though it's not been cut. There is a little dry, spindly grass still there – something for the horses to nibble – but most of their food, certainly that which sustains them, comes out of sacks; corn and so forth. If I cut the field, I doubt I'll take a hundred bales out of it even though it's over four acres. And what's left then, will look like the surface of the moon; not a blade for the horses to eat – unless it rained very soon afterwards, of course."

"Which, of course, is what will happen if the superstition is correct," pointed out Harry Milton, a touch superfluously.

"True, true – but what if it doesn't rain; it would really be a problem then – quite valuable these horses. And I don't need to tell you gentlemen, who've handled livestock all your life, just how delicate, in reality, a horse is. Creatures such as cows and sheep are infinitely tougher and more durable. Give a horse a poor diet, however, and the only beneficiaries are the vets."

"Quite so, Phil – absolutely right. Horses are far more trouble to keep fit and well than anything else on a farm. And I'm sure we understand your reasons for not cutting the grass. To be frank, I suspect we'd all feel as you do had the boot been on the other foot." George Collins got slowly and stiffly to his feet, convinced that his request had fallen on stony ground.

He was wrong. For he had no sooner stood up, with Harry and Arnold following his lead, than Mason had raised a hand to halt them in their tracks. He then got rapidly to his feet himself.

"Just a minute, gentlemen," he implored. "Just a minute; I'm not necessarily saying I will not agree to the cutting of the field. No – not at all. After all, my wife and I are newcomers to the parish – indeed to this lovely county, so we naturally have no desire to upset, or even disappoint, good people like yourselves who have lived here for so long, whose families might well have farmed the land in this parish for generations. No – most certainly not. Also, I'm not a man to pour scorn on superstition, no matter how bizarre it might sound; after all, there is so much in our lives and in this world which defies logical explanation. So, as I say, I'm not ruling out that I might be willing to cut Mary Park. However, my wife and I are partners in the legal as well as the moral sense; thus we usually make joint decisions. So I'm just asking you to let me have, say, a couple of days to talk it over with her, and for us to make a decision on the matter."

"That's fair enough, Phil; of course you will want to discuss it with your wife before making a decision. I would certainly do the same in your position." And George meant every word; he would certainly have discussed such a request with his spouse; in fact he would have viewed such a statement as he had made regarding the cutting of Mary Park with at least, suspicion, probably even credulity. For it was the stuff of medieval witchcraft. "Perhaps we could give you say, forty-eight hours to make a decision. So it's Tuesday evening now – what if we say we'll call on you again early evening on Thursday?"

"Splendid – yes, that's ideal. Clearly it'll give us ample time to decide what we wish to do, but I will not keep you waiting long for an answer. Prevarication is the last thing you want in the present situation – except for the sun of course." He laughed, before speaking again. "So we've two days before Claudia and I have to make a decision as to whether social responsibility should take preference over self-interest. I wonder which will win?"

Likewise did his three visitors, all of them – even the cynical Arnold – now clutching at folklore, hoping that the cutting of the grass on this wretched field of, even at the best of times, relatively poor pasture, could bring about rain and salvation.


The first action taken by Phil Mason after welcoming his three guests on that still sweltering Thursday evening, was to hand out drinks – once more two whiskies and a pint of lager. He raised his own glass and said, softly, "Cheers gentlemen."

Goodly portions of drink having been drained from glasses, the newcomer came, abruptly, to the point of their visit.

"Well, gents, you've come for our decision. We have reached it, although it was not easy. My wife, like myself, is somewhat concerned about the prospect of cutting Mary Park and thus running the risk of leaving our horses with little more than bare ground to tread. They're very important to us, our horses – largely because they are extremely important to our two daughters who are both in their early teens – thirteen and fifteen to be exact."

"So you've decided not to cut it." Arnold Sleeman spoke the words as a statement rather than a question.

Their host shook his head. "On the contrary – Arnold, isn't it? On the contrary, Arnold; I will get it cut in the morning – in theory at least. I've already contacted a local agricultural contractor – we obviously don't have the necessary equipment or implements to fulfil such a task – and I've promised to phone him after you've left this evening to give him the verdict. If we decide to cut it, then he assures me he'll be around before 9am to do it. However, Claudia and I, after giving it much thought, have come up with a condition – a quite modest one to safeguard ourselves in some small way."

"A condition?" George Collins' voice registered a high level of apprehension. Neither he, nor his two colleagues, had pondered that a condition might be attached.

Phil Mason smiled. "Well," said he, "perhaps that's too strong a word. Perhaps wager would be a better description of what we describe. Both of us enjoy a game of chance."

"A game of chance?" Harry Milton, although something of a gambling man in terms of horses and football, was not at all sure that putting a bet down upon something so crucial to their future livelihoods – indeed, their future lives – was a particularly good idea. That apprehension was reflected in his tone of voice.

Mason again smiled, though this time somewhat wanly. "Well, perhaps not altogether a wager as such, gentlemen. It's more that we would like to bring perhaps what could be described as a touch of insurance into our agreement – along with a goodly portion of chance. I'll not beat around the bush; what we propose, Claudia and I, is that I get the contractor in first thing in the morning, as I said just now, and that he cut Mary Park. We will do it as a gesture of neighbourliness to you good folk who face so many problems at present. Now, if after it's been cut, the rain still doesn't come then we'll be in something of the same boat as you farmers – all the farmers in the parish and beyond for that matter. For whilst we'll have a few bales of hay – very few, I fancy, looking at the shortness of the grass – we'll have no grass at all for my horses, just as you have no grass left for your cattle and sheep and so forth. Even then, though, to be fair, we will be better off than you gents; after all, we don't make a living from the land. But if cutting Mary Park really does work – really does activate this extraordinary superstition – and the rains come, then you will all be better off than us. For your stock, your crops, your very livelihood will be saved, whilst all we'll be left with is a field of sodden hay, which, if the rain was to continue – and it might well do, of course – would be ruined. Granted there's not enough in the field to make a great number of bales, but in a year such as this, each single one is both precious and valuable."

He paused, briefly smiled again, and continued.

"So, gentlemen, here's where the element of chance comes in. If the rain does not come within forty-eight hours, as I said just now, we will have tried to break the drought but it will prove, clearly, that the superstition is what could be described as an old wives' tale. If, however, it does rain within forty-eight hours, then you compensate me for the sodden, worthless hay that will be lying on Mary Park. The sum I have in mind is three thousand pounds."

There was a stunned silence which seemed, to Mason, interminable but in reality lasted about thirty seconds. George Collins was the first to speak. "You did say – well, you did say three thousand pounds, Phil – is that right?"

Their host nodded. "Yes, that's correct. Granted it's a tidy sum, but, I feel, in the circumstances, it is a fair suggestion. "But," added he quickly, "I am being a little unfair springing it on you all in this way. Clearly you will want to discuss it, so I'll leave you alone to do so. With time being so vital in this matter, you'll no doubt wish to make a decision here and now. If you do decide to go ahead and take up my offer then, as I intimated just now, I'll ensure that Mary Park is cut tomorrow morning – Friday. If that happens, then should it not rain by, say, noon on Sunday, then you will owe me nothing – even if it rains a minute after that. If, however, it does rain – and I mean, in fairness to you all, measurable rain – then you would owe us three thousand pounds. So gents, I'll leave you for a little while to discuss it and hopefully come to a decision, one way or another. Please call me back in when you have decided – I'll be in the kitchen." With that he swiftly left the room, closing the door behind him.

George shook his head, an expression of bemusement upon his face. "I never thought we'd have to pay him," he muttered.

Arnold shrugged his shoulders. "Well, according to old Tom, they had to pay Farmer Symons compensation for cutting Mary Park back in 1937. And it appears then they had to pay whether it rained or not. At least with this proposition we don't have to fork out if the drought goes on – in fact, even if it went on for another hour after the Sunday noon deadline we wouldn't have to pay."

"You sound like you're willing to pay him, Arnold. It's a tidy sum three thousand pounds, I mean even if it does rain enough to ruin his hay, there would be so few bales there that it wouldn't be worth a tenth of what he's asking. No – it sounds a bit excessive to me."

"Yes," agreed Harry, "it is excessive, or so it seems when considering the value of the paltry amount of hay he would take from the field. Yet, in reality, it would be one thousand pounds from each if us – plenty enough, of course, but not much in the great scheme of things, not if it breaks this blasted drought. I mean, if it rains – really rains, that is – I'll be saved; in fact we all will. Calamity threatens us all – if paying a thousand quid each keeps us in business, then it'll be the best investment any of us will ever make."

Arnold nodded. "Yes – you're right, Harry. It grieves me in a way to pay out what, even in this day and age, is a fair old sum, but if cutting this bloody field makes the grass grow again, then yes, I'll go for it."

The expression upon George Collins' face suggested he was

still unhappy to pay out such a sum. "I can see what you mean, you two – and basically you're right, of course. But it seems to me that if it rains – and we shell out three grand – every farmer in West Devon will gain from it. Perhaps we could get a few others to chip in a bit?"

"It'll not be worth the hassle, George," argued Milton. "Even if we could convince a few that it would be worth their while to have Mary Park cut – and there's a lot of folk about who'll think we've all gone daft believing in such a superstition – it would probably take days to get them on board. We've not that sort of time; if we agree to Mason's terms, he'll get the field cut first thing in the morning – you heard what he said. And we only pay if it rains by noon on Sunday – about forty-eight hours from the time the grass'll be cut. My cattle can survive a couple more days – but precious little after that. No, we either accept Mason's terms here and now – or we forget it."

Harry Milton had put the argument succinctly and clearly.

Arnold slowly nodded his head in agreement. "You're right," he said softly. "We make the decision now – and stick by it. I'm for accepting Mason's terms."

"And I," Harry spoke the two words briskly and decisively. "How about you, George?"

Collins smiled gently. "I'm not happy about having to pay so much – but I take the points you fellows make. I'll make it unanimous – let's go for it." He got to his feet and ambled towards the door. "So I suppose I'd better call him in and tell him we're unanimous for the cutting of Mary Park – on his terms."

Nodded agreement came from his two colleagues; the deal was about to be done.


George Collins drank deep of his pint and placed it back on to the bar. "You know," said he in relaxed fashion, "if truth be told I still can not believe what happened. It's quite, quite unbelievable – like a miracle."

"I believe it, all right," retorted the ancient Tom Wilkins, sat in his usual seat close to the open fireplace in the bar of the

Shepherd's Crook. "In fact, I told you chaps all along that it would work – it always has. Thank heavens you all listened to me. You got that fellow Mason to cut Mary Park, and it has hammered down ever since."

Arnold nodded, as he emptied his glass and handed it to Stan Lawrence to refill, putting a ten pound note on the counter to cover the cost of a round for his two partners in the Mary Park venture, plus one for old Tom and the landlord.

"Well, you're not far out there, Tom," he agreed. "It didn't rain immediately to be strictly accurate, but it did within twelve hours of the cutting. Mason had the field topped about ten o'clock yesterday morning, and by eight o'clock last night it was hammering down – and has done so ever since."

"And is due to carry on doing so," interjected the landlord. "That's what the forecast gave about teatime. In fact, the ground's so hard, and the rain's going to stay so heavy, that they reckon there's a very real chance there could be flooding, with it just running off."

"I wouldn't doubt it," agreed Harry Milton nodding sagely. "I mean, just look at it – it's certainly larruping down. And all because we cut Mary Park – I just can not believe it. One thing for sure, I'll never doubt any superstition ever again."

"Me neither – it's been the best thousand quid I've ever spent," retorted Collins. "Phil Mason looked pleased as punch when I dropped our three cheques round for him this afternoon. He thanked me kindly, asked me to pass on his thanks to you and Arnold, and said that whilst he naturally was happy to receive the three grand, he was truly delighted that this wretched drought is over. He certainly seems a genuine, pleasant sort of chap. He reckons he'll drop in here one evening and buy us all a drink."

"That's the trouble with you farmers," a voice bellowed, "always looking for free drinks – with all the money you lot have got, as well."

Heads turned to see the burly figure of Norman Cooper standing just inside the door of the bar. A butcher by trade, Cooper was a fair advertisement for the meats he sold, being a well built man of some six feet in height – although perhaps a touch too heavy.

"I wish we did have some money, Norman," Arnold retorted. "Still, now that it's started raining we will hopefully be saved from entire ruin."

"Yes – perfectly timed for you chaps, isn't it?" agreed the butcher. "Poor timing from my point of view, though. The fact is this past week I've been starting to fill my freezers with some fair old bargains, reasonably good bullocks being slaughtered cheaply because there was no grass to fill their bellies. And if this drought had gone on, the meat would have been even cheaper, and I'd have bought in enough beef, lamb and pork to keep me going for months. In fact, I'd targeted the next couple of weeks to buy really heavily – the price would have been on the floor, whilst the quality of the stock would still have been reasonable. Anything after that, then the beasts would have been hungry and their condition would have gone back too far – though, of course, they'd have been even cheaper. No, gents, if I'm honest, I'm not at all happy to see this rain." The butcher spoke the words with seriousness – unsympathetic, to say the least, as far as the three farmers were concerned.

"Well Norman, you're honest, I'll give you that," retorted George Collins. "Still, I would have hoped for a little more understanding from a man born and bred in the parish like yourself, who's relied on local meat all your business life." The words had an edge to them; Collins not impressed, to say the least, by the butcher's blatant selfishness.

"It's an ill wind, gentlemen, as the saying goes," stated Cooper. "Still, it's all over now, you can put money on that."

"I reckon it'll rain non-stop 'til Christmas now," opined Stan Lawrence.

"Quite so, Stan," agreed the butcher. "When droughts, or even dry spells, break, then nature – or God perhaps – makes up the balance, and often a bit more. We'll probably reach the end of December and find out that, in total, the year's rainfall locally is higher than the average."

"Yes," said the landlord, "that could well happen. We're certainly due a fair drop in the next week or more; looking at the weather chart on TV this morning, it seems as if there are depressions lined up across the Atlantic like a regiment of soldiers."

"And all of them heading for us. Which, when you think of it, makes it strange that that fellow Mason out at Oaklands Rise cut a field to hay just before it started. Granted, there's not much grass in it, but what little there is will be ruined. Makes no sense when you think of it." The butcher was clearly mystified regarding the cutting of Mary Park.

"Well, that's the way it goes, isn't it; we've all been caught out by the weather over the years – many times, if truth be told." George tried to say the words in as nonchalant a fashion as possible; he, like Arnold and Harry, had no desire to divulge the business deal they had made with Mason based on a superstition. They felt, possibly rightly, that they would be the laughing stock of the parish; and if the butcher heard about it, then the parish would certainly hear of it – not a man to keep things to himself, Norman Cooper.

"Yes, true," agreed Cooper, "but he shouldn't have been caught out like that – Mason, I mean."

"Why not?" Collins asked the question, but the eyes and ears of the other two farmers were also firmly fixed on Cooper's mouth, awaiting his explanation, an awareness growing upon them that the butcher appeared to know something which they did not.

"Well, it's obvious surely," retorted Cooper. "I mean, weather's his job, isn't it."

"How do you mean, weather's his job?" The landlord asked the question, the three farmers becoming increasingly alarmed as to what they were going to hear.

"Well, he's a met man, isn't he," stated the butcher in a tone of voice which suggested he felt he was talking to idiots. "Surely you knew that. I thought that was well known in the parish. He works at the met office in Exeter – his missus as well. That's what makes it so strange he should have cut Mary Park. After all, he would have known there was rain on the way. Daft, isn't it, to cut a field of grass when you know it's going to rain."

# II

# The 'At

Arthur Bowman adjusted his new headgear – the 'at being an expected, but none too welcome Christmas gift from his practical wife – took a deep breath then marched forward and unbolted the door of his shop. Though it was New Year's Eve, with business good and folk, generally, in a festive mood, he still anticipated a fraught day.

He glanced outside the door; nobody around at present, but they soon would be. Mrs Bailey would be in for certain, and before nine. He went back behind the counter, put his knife to the quarter of beef laying before him on the slab, and dismembered it with a skill perfected during more than forty years in the trade.

He heard the door open and close, felt a momentary blast from an uncompromising north-easterly blowing straight off Dartmoor, and swung around to see the corpulent figure of Lily Bailey standing before him.

She looked surprised. "Why, Mr Bowman," she cried, "I 'ardly recognised you in your new 'at. I don't ever recall seeing you in an 'at before. It looks – well – strange to see you in an 'at."

"Not my idea, missus," grunted the butcher. "It's the 'ealth inspector. Menace 'ee is; been after me for years to make all sorts of changes in the shop. Nonsense most of 'em. After all, me and my father before me 'ave sold meat from this shop for the best part of sixty years without all the daft rubbish in the shop this council man says I've got to 'ave installed. And nobody 'as ever been took bad, 'ave they? Our meat's always been as good as you could buy in all of Devon – isn't that so?"

"Well, I've never 'ad cause for complaint," the customer conceded.

"Exactly. But that's not enough for this council fellah. 'Ee's been on at me for some time to do this, that and the other, and 'ee said to me last week that if I didn't make a start on things within a fortnight, and begin wearing an 'at by the New Year, 'ee'd take me to court – saucy devil."

"What 'ave you got to do?"

"Well, mainly, I've got to put a washbasin in the corner of the shop so I can wash me 'ands regular and 'ave one of they new electric things that kills flies. Can't see anything wrong with the old sticky papers, myself, but 'ee says they're not i'genic. Nonsense. Still, I've got to do that and one or two other things besides – including wearing this 'at, of course. Makes me wild, but you can't beat 'em. They've got the whip 'and. Took a butcher in Plymouth to court a few months back for not wearing 'is 'at, they did. 'Ee was fined a fair bit, too. Police state, that's what it is."

"Well, I must say it all sounds a bit unnecessary," agreed Mrs Bailey, putting her regular order of a pound of pasty meat into her shopping bag, the imminent New Year celebrations not altering her buying habits in any way. "And I must say Mr Bowman, that an 'at doesn't really suit you; a happy New Year to you."

With that she was gone, leaving a bemused butcher in her wake. He shook his head sadly, then returned to his quarter of beef. He had no sooner picked up his knife, though, than a discordant bellow rent the air, and caused him to jerk his head around.

"What 'ave 'ee got on yer 'ead, Arthur?" was the booming question asked, to be followed by a raucous guffaw. "Just as well you got big yers, boy, or else the old 'at 'ud be down over your eyes," continued the abuse. But then, nothing other than such an outburst could be expected from Bert Lanyon, long considered the 'mouth' of the village.

"Still, if it baint affecting yer cutting 'and, I'll 'ave a couple of pork chops," came the instruction.

The butcher went about his business, giving the same explanation as he had to Mrs Bailey, as he did so. The customer took his chops, paid his money, then delivered his parting shot; "They wouldn't make me wear an 'at if I didn't want to. Have a good New Year, Arthur."

And so it went on throughout a long and very busy morning, his wearing of an 'at bringing reactions from his loyal customers ranging from incredulity to plain merriment, whilst he almost exhausted himself repeatedly giving his rather involved explanation. By noon, he'd had enough of both receiving comments and giving explanations, so he removed his 'at, hurled it into the cupboard under the counter, and swore never to wear it again.

He certainly didn't sport it when the Health Inspector visited again immediately after the New Year break – as he had promised to do. A keen, ambitious young fellow, he had no sooner entered the shop, wishing the proprietor a brisk, "Good morning," than his eyes were darting around the place to see if his instructions had been obeyed.

"I see you have not installed the washbasin," he said, in clipped tones.

"It's all in 'and," grunted Bowman. "I'm just waiting for a quote from Dave Dawkins, the plumber. There's no rush, is there?" he asked, aggressively.

"Well, I do feel the work should be carried out as soon as possible. And the insect killer – I see no sign of that either."

"That's in 'and, as well. Freddie Coleman the electrician's getting one for me. 'Ee's 'ad to order it from up the line somewhere. There's nothing more I can do about either of these things other than what I've already done. It's always hard to get things done this time of the year as you must surely realise. After all, most of the country's been liquored up for a fortnight or so, and will be for the best part of another week yet."

"That's as may be, Mr Bowman," retorted the official, sharply, "but there's something you can do immediately about the hat which the regulations require. I see you've still not got one."

"That's where you're wrong then – I 'ave; the only thing is, I refuse to wear it."

"But why?"

"Because I look a right fool. In fact, everybody laughs at me in it."

"Oh come now, Mr Bowman, I'm sure that's not true. But even if it is, people will soon get used to it – as will you. It really is important you wear it."

"Why? You never did tell me why. Only that I 'ad to wear one."

"For hygiene reasons, of course. It stops your hair falling into the meat."

"Me 'air?" he rasped. "Did you say, me 'air? Are you blind – or just plain daft? Look at me 'ead – I 'aven't got any 'air. I'm bald as a badger." He pointed to his shiny pate. " 'Ave been since I was twenty-five years old."

"I appreciate that, Mr Bowman," replied the official, "but the law is the law, and must be obeyed."

"Not when it's plain daft." The butcher was looking angry now, his face the colour of the beef on the slab. And that fury showed as he strode aggressively from behind the counter to confront the official standing in the middle of the shop, his clipboard held in front of him like a shield.

Bowman stood before the young man, pushed his face to within six inches of his increasingly worried looking countenance, and said in a controlled but somewhat threatening voice, "Right, my friend, let's get down to brass tacks. You've spent a fair bit of time telling me what I must do; now I'm telling you what I intend to do. I will put the washbasin in because I fancy it'll be an 'andy thing to 'ave in the shop; I'll 'ave the fly thing as well because I don't think they make fly papers as good as they used to. But whilst I'll not get rid of me 'at, I won't wear it either – it'll stay where it is, in the cupboard. So both of us'll be satisfied then; I'll 'ave an 'at, like you say I've got to, but I won't make meself look a fool by wearing it. All right?"

The final word was expressed in as belligerent and threatening a tone as the young health inspector had ever heard, and just the slightest glance at Arthur Bowman's ferocious expression was sufficient to convince him that the butcher, at moments such as these, was a dangerous man to deal with.

The official, essentially a retiring man, felt that the best thing he could do at this moment was to do just that – retire from this confrontation.

He quickly nodded his agreement to Bowman's terms, bade the butcher a mumbled "Good morning," added, with a kind of fearful courtesy, "a happy New Year to you," and fled from the shop, never to return. And Arthur Bowman, always a man of his word, never did again wear his 'at.

# III

# The Carnival

Greater calamities than the cancellation of the annual Carnival could befall the folk of Brendon Combe – but not many. For over forty years the town had sported a Carnival procession – always on the second Saturday of September – and for a generation now it had been as good as anything Devon could produce. In fact, the previous year, for the first time, over forty lorry borne floats were involved in the procession, as well as numerous walking entries, which had made the event a fine spectacle and had brought large crowds thronging to the town – a welcome, indeed, vital bonanza for shops, pubs, restaurants and the numerous charities that always benefited from the generosity of people in happy, relaxed mood.

The success of the Carnival, however, had become ever more dependent upon the availability of lorries to carry the myriad, and often massive, floats – which is where Aubrey Dalton came in. For this good man – Brendon Combe born – having taken over his father's small haulage firm some three decades earlier and built it into one of the largest freight companies in the South West, had over the years provided, totally free of charge, an ever increasing number of lorries for the carrying of the floats, an annual gesture of extreme generosity. In fact the number of Dalton wagons the previous year had been thirty-three, so without them the Carnival, simply, would not take place.

As the Carnival Committee came to order in the back room of

46

The Fur and Ferret, under the chairmanship of Frank Blackmore, this was the catastrophe which confronted them – and the town. For Aubrey Dalton, the previous day, had informed Blackmore that none of his lorries would be available for the procession this year, which meant, with a mere ten days remaining before the Carnival, for the first time since its inception it might have to be cancelled.

The trouble was caused by a woman – as always, according to bachelor Blackmore. For Aubrey Dalton – a widower – had remarried some twelve months earlier, and had not, according to local wisdom, married wisely. His new bride was nothing but a 'gold digger', it was said, and in Aubrey she had most assuredly found a lucrative 'lode'. What was fact, however, was that the new Mrs Dalton, Linda by name, was almost thirty years younger than her husband, who was in his mid-sixties. About two years previously she had come to live in the village, from London it was believed – though little was known of her background. An attractive woman with a good line in chat, she had, in the opinion of most local folk, seen Aubrey – vulnerable after the sudden death of his dear wife Edna, again about two years back – as a 'good catch'.

And catch him she did – and he, being besotted with her, was ruled by the woman.

Thus came about his estrangement with Brendon Combe Carnival Committee. For a couple of evenings previously, there was held in the town hall the annual selection of the Carnival Queen. There were nine entrants – all between the ages of twelve and sixteen in accordance with the rules – but there was never any doubt that the winner would be Vicky, the beautiful and vivacious daughter of Jack Miller, conductor and secretary of the Town Band. One girl who had not the slightest chance of the crown was Marie Lewis, the new stepdaughter of Aubrey Dalton. A pleasant and intelligent girl, Marie was rather plain – though at only thirteen years of age she had plenty of time to 'blossom' – and had no illusions about the fact. Nor did she have any desire to be the Carnival Queen and had only entered at her mother's insistence.

Linda Dalton, however, saw things very differently. She was furious that these 'peasants' could choose some 'skinny kid' as Carnival Queen when they could have had her daughter. Unfortunately, with Linda fury, invariably, turned into vindictiveness; so she demanded of her husband that he refuse the Carnival the use of any of his lorries. Aubrey was appalled at this and initially refused to do it. His wife persisted, however, and Aubrey, aware that their marriage was not prospering as it should have been and thus anxious to appease this demanding woman – whom, rumour had it, had been seen on occasions in the company of another man at the local golf club – caved in and informed Blackmore that all his lorries would be withdrawn, and the reason for it.

So the necessity for a crisis meeting of the Committee – which was confrontational and largely defeatist. Myriad solutions where thrown in the ring, from the simple one of cancelling the Carnival to the blatantly appeasing move of taking the crown away from Vicky Miller and giving it to Marie Lewis. This solution might well have been agreed upon had it not been pointed out that if Jack Miller's daughter ceased to be Carnival Queen then he most assuredly would cease to bring the Town Band to play at the Carnival, which would have been another calamity. So the quest for a way to get Aubrey Dalton to relent resumed – at enormous length.

Just when it appeared to be insoluble, Alice Benson, the oldest member of the Committee came up with a suggestion. "When I was a girl," she mused, "we always used to have a May Fair in Brendon Combe – and a May Queen, of course. Perhaps we could revive that, and make Marie the May Queen?" One far too logical member of the Committee made the point that it was plain daft to have a May Queen in September, but he was ignored. The overwhelming majority of the fourteen people gathered thought it a brilliant idea – and it was rapidly adopted. A float would be knocked up, a costume created and Marie Lewis would be the May Queen. Frank Blackmore agreed to take the great news to the Daltons the very next day and do his best to ensure such tidings brought about a change of heart in the lorry owner – and, more especially, in his formidable wife.

So the next morning found the Chairman of the Carnival Committee on the ample doorstep of the Daltons' superb house on the edge of town, ringing the bell. After what seemed an age, Aubrey opened the door and stood before him – a sorry sight indeed. For the man appeared to have aged ten years, was unshaven and still clad in pyjamas and dressing gown even though it was past ten in the morning. He saw Blackmore standing before him, but appeared not to notice his polite "Good morning." Rather, he muttered softly:

"She's gone, Frank. Gone and shacked up with some fellow from Torquay, she has. Met him at the Golf Club, apparently. Owns several hotels – plenty of money. And that's all she's interested in – money. Took the little maid with her; good little maid, is Marie. Worth ten of her mother," he added venomously. He shook his head wearily; "What a fool I've been, boy. It's true though, isn't it – there's no fool like an old fool. All she wanted from me was my money."

Frank was about to mouth his solicitations and then move on to the subject which had brought about his visit, when suddenly Dalton erupted:

"Money!" he roared. "Of course, money – what a fool I am; she's my wife, my heir. She stands to inherit virtually all I've got."

He turned to go back into the house, saying, "I've got to phone my solicitor right away, Frank. There's not a minute to lose, I've got to make sure she gets not a penny piece of mine."

He was about to disappear back into the house when Blackmore did the only thing he could in the circumstances. Well aware that exceptional needs gave justification to exceptional acts – he stepped over the doorstep, grabbed Aubrey Dalton by the right shoulder, spun him round, and rasped, "The lorries, Aubrey – will you let us have the lorries for the Carnival?"

Dalton looked totally bemused and for several seconds said not a word. Then he merely shrugged his shoulders, nodded his head and said, "Of course. I always supply the lorries for the Carnival. You ought to know that, Frank; after all, you are the Chairman."

c

# IV

# The Martyr

Jack Dixon JP walked slowly across the ancient square towards the equally historic courthouse on the far side, tightening his overcoat about him as he went. It was only early October – not yet Goose Fair day – but there was definitely a feeling of winter in the air, with a fine chill drizzle down from off Dartmoor. The courtroom would be cold for certain, even if they had the archaic heating system turned on.

The bench had been told two or three years earlier that new, fully modern central heating units were to be installed after an elderly lady sitting at the back of the courtroom had been rushed to hospital with hypothermia, having come in to give moral support to her grandson who was due to be sentenced for assault. The problem had been that she had to wait most of the morning simply because the lad – who had spent far too much of his young life in trouble – hadn't turned up by 10am as instructed. Thus his gran had to wait patiently until noon when the court had completed its list just in case he did come. He did not, a warrant for his arrest was issued, and the usher, who knew the lady quite well because of her regular court attendance, went to inform her of what was happening.

Fortunately she recovered quite quickly, and had made further appearances in the court to witness the law deal with both her grandsons, the younger one having joined his dysfunctional brother in pursuing a life of crime. However these appearances had all been during spring or summer.

The subject of the central heating had been brought up at a previous bench meeting – on a baking day in June – when their senior legal adviser, Malcolm Naylor, had assured them that a new system would be installed before winter – "of which year?" enquired one magistrate, sardonically.

Dixon opened the side door between the courtroom and police station, closed it behind him, and slowly ascended the granite, unforgiving spiral staircase to the retiring room above. Pulling open the heavy, studded door, he entered the spacious room – which felt a little warmer than normal. As he entered the room, the door opposite – which went into the court – also opened to enable the entrance of the long serving, pleasant and most able usher, Alison Coleman.

"Morning, Mrs Coleman." Jack greeted the lady with genuine warmth, for she was a person for whom he – and every member of the bench – had the highest regard; for there seemed to be no situation which could arise amongst the myriad and volatile clientele which frequented the Court, that she seemed unable to handle. The arrogant were made humble, the stressed put at their ease, the potentially violent pacified, the troubled counselled; she was social worker, probation officer, policeman and Samaritan all rolled into one – a remarkable woman.

"Good morning, Mr Dixon," she replied. "I've put the coffee to percolate" – she pointed towards the small table at the far side of the room – "and I've bought a packet of Fox's Chocolate Selection biscuits; I saw you were sitting today and I know they're your favourites."

The magistrate grinned. "You're good to me, Mrs Coleman; it is appreciated even though it does me no good, if I'm honest," said he, tapping a more than adequate midriff. "Mind you, I will share them with my two colleagues when they arrive – although I fancy a few of these could well go down the red lane before they get here." He grabbed a brace of chocolate covered shortbread as he spoke.

"Well, I always feel, Mr Dixon, that you magistrates give of your time for nothing, so the least the court can do is provide you with a decent cup of coffee and a few good quality biscuits. Fortunately I managed to convince Mr Naylor of this, so I'm getting a reasonable amount out of petty cash each week to buy good coffee, tea and biscuits."

"Money well spent," replied the magistrate.

The usher turned and moved back towards the door. "Well I'd better be off – there are several attendees, quite a few solicitors, and there are some reporters here as well – not local ones either. And looking out of the window just now, I'm sure I saw a television crew. Heaven knows what that's all about – I've not had the list from Mr Naylor as yet. There must be something a little unusual though." With that she was across the room and through the door, swiftly, as was her way, her black gown billowing a little from her tall, slender figure.

Dixon ate, rapidly, the two biscuits, then poured himself a cup of black coffee, and took another brace of biscuits from the packet. He sat down at the large table which dominated the room, then glanced at his watch. It was still not quite 9.30 – more than half an hour before the court commenced. It was very much his routine to be early, though; in fact he was almost invariably the first to arrive. He liked to sit for a while, on his own, drinking some coffee or tea, eating some of Mrs Coleman's biscuits – for some reason, he always found it relaxing. He had spent a few minutes alone with his thoughts when he heard the door open. He turned to see Max Burton entering the room – puffing just a little after having scaled the steps; like Dixon, he was a man in middle age who carried just a few pounds too many.

"Morning, Max."

"Good to see you, Jack," came the reply – a little breathlessly.

Dixon got up from his seat, and went over to the percolator. "Coffee, Max?"

"Please – milk and two sugars. And I'll help myself to a handful of those biscuits as well; Fox's – take a bit of beating they do. Good old Alison – wonderful woman, that. Do you know that a couple of weeks ago, I sat at the Crown court on an appeal; there wasn't a biscuit in sight and you had to pay for coffee."

"Pay for coffee?" The information stunned Jack Dixon. In fact he said the words in such a tone as to suggest that it was possibly the most outrageous extortion he had heard of in all his fifty-three years. "That's – that's – that's appalling."

Burton nodded agreement, his mouth full of biscuit. It took but a few seconds to empty it though, whereupon he said, "I don't know what's on today, but there are TV cameras outside."

"Yes – and several reporters inside, according to Alison. She was going to find out what it's all about. It must be something quite high profile. It always makes me a bit nervous, though, when the media are here mob handed. It means that whatever it is, we've got to get it right."

His colleague nodded agreement, his mouth again packed with biscuit.

Dixon emptied his cup, went to the table, refilled his cup, took another biscuit, and returned to his seat. He eyed his companion who was just swallowing the last of his mouthful. "I forgot to look at the rota for today Max, and I've not brought it with me. Do you know who we're sitting with this morning?"

His companion nodded – then raised his eyebrows in a gesture of despair. "Molly Francis," said he in melancholy tones.

"Oh – no. I think I'd have gone sick if I'd known that. She's a shocker – and she doesn't ever appear to get any better."

"Sadly, you're right," agreed his companion. "I hope there are no 'not guilty' pleas this morning. I mean if she had been judging Harold Shipman, she'd not have convicted him. 'He seems such a nice man' – that's what she would have said, I bet. I've been on the bench for twenty-odd years, but I've never met anybody like her. I mean, it's not just she refuses to find people guilty, it's that even if they plead 'guilty', she never really wants to punish them – certainly, she's always against sending anybody to prison, no matter how big a thug they might be."

"True," said Jack, nodding his head briskly. "She considers it almost a savage sentence when we put somebody on probation. And as to that about finding people guilty, when I sat with her the other week we had a chap plead guilty to assault, only for her not to believe him, even though he'd been convicted four times previously for it. She reckoned he only pleaded guilty because he didn't want the hassle of a trial. She really is a nightmare."

"She is that. Yet, as a person, she's extremely nice. In fact in the personal sense she is very pleasant indeed – a very likeable woman. She's an awful magistrate, though; I don't know how she was appointed."

Jack was just about to speculate as to why Molly Francis had become the twelfth and most recent member of the bench a couple of years earlier, when the door opened and the lady herself entered.

"Morning, Molly," they chorused, somewhat sheepishly. Still, the door leading to the stairwell was that thick it was most unlikely she could have overheard any part of their conversation.

"Coffee or tea, Molly?"

"Coffee, Jack, please. White, no sugar."

Handing her the cup of coffee, he enquired, "Biscuit?"

"No thanks – far too fattening," – words spoken by a woman who was as slim as a reed. "Have we got much on today?" She addressed herself to Dixon as he was chairing the triumvirate who were sitting that morning.

"I don't know to be honest, Molly. There's certainly something afoot, mind you, with all this media presence. There's got to be something out of the ordinary – or somebody."

Before any further speculation could take place, the door leading from the court opened, and the tall, very thin figure of Malcolm Naylor appeared, his expression, as ever, one of lugubrious gravity. A courteous, kindly and competent man, the legal adviser to the bench exuded an air of melancholy – and had done so throughout the dozen or so years he had been attached to the bench.

"Good morning, Your Worships," said he in sepulchral tones, with a slight bow – one of the old school in terms of deference, was Naylor.

His greeting was returned by the trio who sat in front of him, before Jack Dixon got briskly to the point. "Why are we cursed with the media this morning, Mr Naylor. Not that there's anything wrong with the local papers mind you – in fact I like to see the court covered locally; after all, that's local justice being seen to be done. But it appears we've got them from all over today – TV as well."

"And radio too," replied the legal adviser. "We have the full range of media here today – including the nationals."

"It's the Helen Harding case – that comes up later this morning."

"Oh, no – not today, is it?" Max Burton put his hands to his face as he spoke the words. "I didn't realise it was today. Clearly the money's not been paid – she wouldn't be here else."

"Quite correct, Mr Burton," confirmed Naylor. "Nothing has been paid, I'm afraid."

"I forgot it was this morning that her case came up again," muttered Dixon, half to himself. "I should have remembered 'cause I was Chairman of the bench that sentenced her to twenty-one days in jail unless she paid by today. How I forgot that, I really do not know."

"She obviously wishes to go to prison, Your Worship, for she has just arrived at court with a small suitcase. Sadly that was ever the intention, I feel – she wishes to be a martyr."

Molly Francis looked most confused. "What's this all about?" asked she. "It's the first I've heard of this case."

"This lady, Helen Harding, is an elderly person, Mrs Francis – eighty-one years old to be exact," explained the legal adviser in his patient but pained manner. "She lives here in the town. During the district council's last financial year, which terminated at the end of last March – more than six months ago, now – she made a protest against the council's survey into the treatment received by the ethnic, gay and lesbian minorities in the area. It was stated in the local press that the survey cost several thousand pounds to carry out; Mrs Harding, who objected very strongly to such a survey, somehow decided that the amount of her total council tax payment for the year spent upon this survey, was seventy pounds. Thus, in protest, she deducted this amount from the total due to the council, and sent them a cheque for the remainder. Such a sum, in reality, was far more than would have been her individual contribution to this survey but that, in law, has no relevance. If it had only been seventy pence she had held back, the council would still have taken her to court – they have a statutory duty to do so. Four weeks ago today, after many court appearances by Mrs Harding and consistent refusals to pay the seventy pounds to the council – who incidentally could have asked for interest on the outstanding sum, and considerable costs for all the time put to this case by their legal department, but have not, simply demanding from this lady the initial seventy pounds – the bench, of which Mr Dixon was chairman, took what I feel was the only course open to them; they sentenced Mrs Harding to twenty-one days imprisonment unless the money was paid before her court appearance this morning. Unfortunately no money has been received."

"So we'll have to bang her up for three weeks," stated Dixon, his face looking even graver than Naylor's. "We've no option. The trouble is though, we'll be slaughtered by the media. I can see the headlines now – eighty-one year old woman sent to prison for seventy pounds. The whole thing's a nightmare; I really don't know how I forgot about it."

"We can't – we mustn't send her to prison," cried Molly Francis. "It's ludicrous – we must give her a – well – a conditional discharge, even an absolute discharge; something after that fashion. We can not send an old lady like her to prison – it would be inhuman."

"Unfortunately, ma'am, we've no option," opined the legal adviser. "Twenty-one days' imprisonment was not stated twenty-eight days ago as a sentencing option or possibility or anything of that nature; rather it was a formal sentence. Mrs Harding was sentenced to twenty-one days imprisonment if the sum of seventy pounds was not paid; it has not been, it seems it is unlikely it will be paid in the little time we have this morning, so the prison sentence has to be activated. Mind you, it's probable she'll only do half the sentence, which is standard procedure."

"No, we've no option – true," agreed Max Burton. "And she'll enjoy it – as will the media, like you said Jack. She'll spend ten or eleven days in jail – she'll only serve about half her sentence – and that probably in the hospital wing, then come out and sell her story to the *Sun* or *News of the World* or some-such paper.

We'll be villains, but she'll be a heroine – and a fair bit richer, as well."

"Spot on, Max," agreed the chairman. "I wish there was a way around it, but I fancy there isn't." He lapsed into silence for a few seconds, an idea beginning to germinate in his generally fertile brain.

This silence was punctuated, rapidly, by Molly Francis. "This is dreadful – truly dreadful. I really cannot be involved in doing this – it is so, so, so unjust. If we do this, then I shall have to consider my future as a magistrate; I will feel so guilty, even despicable, sending an elderly lady to prison on a matter of principle and conscience."

"It's not principle though, is it – or conscience," Burton argued (in the back of his mind the thought growing that if Molly did resign, then at least, something positive would have been gained from the day). "No – it's cussedness and bloody-mindedness, and, frankly, it speaks of intolerance against minority groups. "The last few words were an afterthought, but he felt them to be useful words to be used against a magistrate who believed in most things being tolerated, no matter how bizarre they might be. "I reckon there's scarcely a person in the entire district who does not object to some aspect or other of council expenditure. Yet we all pay it – the vast majority of us, at least – because if we did not, we would have chaos, anarchy even. No, if we send her to jail today, she will deserve it – because she will have deliberately brought it upon herself."

"Is she the first case on, Mr Naylor?" enquired the chairman, somewhat tersely.

"No – probably the last, sir. It's just that if her case is put to the end of the list, it will not be heard until late morning – possibly even this afternoon, as we've quite a lot of work to get through this morning. I feel that the later it comes up, the better, for it'll do Mrs Harding no harm to be kept waiting for her to act her role of martyr; also there is the chance that some members of the media might get fed up with waiting, thus abandon the court – and their lurid story."

"Good thinking," concurred the chairman. He got to his feet;

"If you would all excuse me for a couple of minutes – I've an urgent call I must make on my mobile." No sooner had he said the words than he was going out through the heavy door which led to the staircase. Closing it behind him, he dialled the number of his newsagent's shop and spoke with his wife, Sandy.

True to his word, he was back in the retiring room within two minutes and ready for the briefing as to the clientele they would be dealing with that day.

"It's going to be a busy morning, Your Worships, as I intimated just now. There are several attendees and also we have four in custody, three men and a woman."

"Four – the police must have been busy for a change," rasped Max Barton, never a great admirer of the competence or industry of the local constabulary.

"Well, to start with we have a serving prisoner from Dartmoor – he hit another prisoner over the head with a fire extinguisher. Nasty business – the victim is in intensive care at Derriford Hospital at present. It will be at least a charge of grievous bodily harm – perhaps even of attempted murder. And criminal damage, of course."

"Criminal damage?" enquired Dixon.

"Yes – to the fire extinguisher – badly dented, apparently. Quite valuable items, of course. It'll be a straight remand in custody to appear again to be committed to Plymouth Crown Court. There is also a young woman named Sophie Gibson – lives here in the town. She was arrested last night at the burger stall in the Square for taking a knife to the fellow who runs it because he somehow managed to squirt ketchup on her new white top. I'm not sure yet with what she'll be charged, but carrying an offensive weapon will certainly be amongst the charges."

"That could be described as something of an over reaction," grunted Burton.

"Probably she was stressed," opined Molly Francis. "I can understand it to a degree – a new top, then suddenly it is ruined. An understandable reaction in a way – although a little over the top, I would have to concede."

Her male colleagues gazed at her in astonishment, but were

prevented from uttering disbelief at what she had just said by the sharp and timely intervention of their legal adviser.

"Her solicitor will ask for bail, but the Crown Prosecution Service will oppose that most strongly. There will be an application by the prosecution that she be remanded for a week for them to decide on the actual charges to bring. Then there's young Johnny Miller," continued Naylor, somewhat more briskly than was his usual style, aware that every minute would be vital if the court was to finish by lunchtime, which, he surmised was probably the ambition of the bench (it usually was), and was certainly his as an afternoon spent upon the golf course called loud and clear.

"The police arrested him yesterday on a warrant issued a couple of weeks ago – fine defaulter; he owes £720. Motoring offences, of course – it always is with him. The last time he attended was to explain why he'd not been paying at all. Anyway, the last time he was in – two months ago now – he was told that it was his last chance. He's not paid, Your Worships, so if I may suggest, respectfully, a suspended sentence should be put on him. If he fails to pay in future – even for one week – then he will be arrested and taken to Exeter Prison to serve whatever term you decide to impose today."

"How much does that much debt carry?" the chairman enquired.

"Forty-two days, sir," came the instant reply – Malcolm Naylor had been doing this job for so long that such basic questions as sentencing guidelines were as simple as the three times table.

"Sounds like a sensible way forward. We'll have to listen to what he's got to say, of course – but that'll be a load of old nonsense, you may depend." Jack Dixon had been listening to such tales for a very long time.

"It could be that he has a genuine reason for not having paid. Some of these young people lead such disorganised lives that they find it most difficult to fall in with the rules which society lays down. It could be that he needs just a little more time to get himself sorted out," opined Molly.

"More time?" Max Burton uttered the words in a state of bemused exasperation – a regular emotion of his when sitting with Molly Francis. "For heaven's sake, he's . . ."

He got no further, for Malcolm Naylor, a past master at interrupting magistrates without ever appearing to be rude, cut him off, rapidly, before he could get into an entertaining, but time consuming rant (very good at those, was Max – something of which the long serving Naylor was most aware). "I have to say, Mrs Francis, that Mr Burton is absolutely correct," he articulated, urbanely. "This young man has been treated with great tolerance and fairness by a number of benches in the past three or four years. I would say that only the threat of imprisonment is likely to produce regular payment of what is a considerable sum – and even then I would be surprised if he does not fail to pay on a regular basis. Still, time marches on – our fourth prisoner is Danny Durban."

"Now there's a surprise," retorted Jack Dixon. "Violence, I presume?"

"Unfortunately, yes, sir. You may recall that about a month ago, when in custody for attacking the landlord of the Tavy Arms, you gave him a non-custodial sentence – a final chance, you said, to sort himself out."

"Yes, that's right," agreed the chairman. "I was sitting that day – although I don't believe you two were," said he, addressing his colleagues. "A community punishment order, and attendance at an anger management course – I think that was our sentence, Mr Naylor."

"Indeed it was, sir. Two hundred hours' work in the community and, as you said, attendance once a week, for three months at an anger management course."

"So, what's he done now?"

"Assaulted his anger management counsellor, I'm afraid. Broke his nose. It's GBH this time. He'll be represented as always by Julian Higgins, who told me just now he will be making a bail application, although the way he said it, he doesn't expect it to be granted. Clearly he is only making it at the insistence of his client."

"No, I don't think chances of bail are great, I must say," agreed Max Burton, with the dry chuckle which was very much his own.

"Well, I see no reason why we should not give him bail," Molly Francis interjected. "After all, as we are constantly being told, we should seek to keep people out of prison, only sentencing them to custody when clearly there is no alternative. Anyway, everybody has the right to apply for bail, and everybody has the right to a fair hearing; that's what English Justice and Common Law is based upon, isn't that so?" She spoke the last few words with, if not aggression exactly, certainly, for her, an unusual amount of assertiveness in her tone.

Jack Dixon was anxious to appease her, always keen, when in the chair, to lead a happy and contented team. "Quite right, Molly," agreed he. "Clearly he has the right, through his solicitor, to make such an application – and he will be given a fair hearing. That's all the custody cases, Mr Naylor – what others have we?"

The chairman was anxious to take the conversation away from the subject of Danny Durban's bail application – it was nearing ten o'clock, when the sitting was due to start, and their legal adviser had still to brief them on myriad other cases coming before the court that day.

"We've a few general motoring offences, sir – a couple attending – but mostly postal pleas of guilty. We've one excess alcohol – a fellow four and a half times over the limit. The police say they had to hold him up to give him a breath test. He is going to plead not guilty."

"Not guilty," Molly Francis's voice was shrill with incredulity; drink driving was one of the very, very few offences which she saw as being serious, and was rarely even remotely sympathetic to the accused.

"He admits he had been drinking," replied Naylor, in his habitual level, unemotional tone, "but claims that he was too drunk to blow into the breathalyser correctly; thus, his submission is that it would have been impossible for the breathalyser to register anything at all, let alone four and a half times over the limit."

"You cannot be serious. You mean to say he is pleading not

guilty on these grounds? That's ludicrous – more, it's an insult to our intelligence." Dixon shook his head in despair.

"Clearly it is," agreed their legal adviser. "He is not yet legally represented, so I've suggested to him that he has a word with Mr Higgins, who is duty solicitor today – and take some advice from him before formally entering a plea. Apart from these cases, we've only got the Jenkins brothers in, charged with poaching salmon in the Tamar – a not guilty plea, of course, as it always is with them – so we'll have to fix a trial date this morning; also we've a dangerous dog case, again a not guilty plea."

"Ever thus, isn't it, with dangerous dogs – a not guilty plea, I mean," opined Burton, his voice dominated by cynicism. "I don't think I ever recall anybody accused of owning a dangerous dog pleading guilty. I reckon whoever owned the Hound of the Baskervilles would have pleaded not guilty to having a dangerous animal; they would probably have said that the beast had a loving nature and was merely playing at the time."

Malcolm Naylor gave one of his rare, and wry, smiles, then nodded. "There is much truth in that, sir," he agreed. "For not only do people plead not guilty, they appear, almost invariably, to be offended that any creature owned by them, or under their control, can ever be deemed dangerous, or, indeed, even remotely anti-social." He shook his head, an expression of world weariness flitting across his features, to be replaced rapidly by his customary lugubriousness. "That is about it, Your Worships – except, of course, for our friend Helen Harding whom, as I intimated just now, I plan to put to the end of the list. It'll not harm her to have to wait two or three hours for her martyrdom – it'll be longer, of course, should we have to go into the afternoon. And some of the media might just get sufficiently impatient before then to cause them to abandon their stay. I am a touch doubtful if I'm frank, but we can but hope, at least."

The legal adviser glanced at his watch. "It's a minute past ten – the court is ready when you are, Your Worships." He inclined his head as he spoke the words, and had soon exited through the door which accessed the courtroom.

Within thirty seconds, the magistrates had followed him, and taken their place on the raised dais at the end of the Victorian built courtroom. A grade one listed building, it was a bleak place, with hard, uncompromising benches, high, slightly discoloured ceilings and inadequate lighting. As usual, it was several degrees colder than it was outside, the archaic central heating system – which, for years, was always going to be replaced 'next summer' – being virtually useless.

Molly Francis – who often described herself as a 'cold bird' – shivered as she took her place on the hard seat, with the chairman beside her and Max Burton on the far side of him. She leant down and switched on the heater which lay down in front of the bench, attached to the back of the high desk upon which they could lean, and masked the veteran, and none too efficient, heaters which would keep their legs warm, if little else. Inefficient though these heaters were, the magistrates still enjoyed a slightly warmer experience than did those in all other parts of the courtroom.

Jack Dixon looked about him, and took in a goodly number of clients and spectators sitting in the serried rows of benches towards the back of the court, their numbers augmented by a posse of journalists – into double figures – who were surplus to a press bench that would accommodate only four, that generally being more than adequate. The chairman uttered a brisk, "Good morning," to the audience, all standing in accordance with custom, then sat down, everyone else doing likewise.

"Perhaps, Your Worships, we may begin with those in custody," intoned the legal adviser – which is what they did. The Dartmoor prisoner – built like Lennox Lewis – appeared briefly, to be further remanded in custody, with the instruction he be brought before the court four weeks hence, when he would be formally committed to the Crown Court for trial – or, if he pleaded 'guilty', merely for sentencing, the latter being the most likely as there were at least a dozen witnesses, many of them fellow inmates, who had seen him commit the offence. Whatever, it was a virtual certainty that he would be spending somewhat longer at the notorious old prison than he had anticipated when being sentenced to two years some nine months previously.

The young local woman, Sophie Gibson, who had brandished

the knife at the burger stall was told she would remain in custody despite an eloquent plea for bail from her solicitor, an up and coming young fellow called Simon Strong, who had recently come to live and work in the town. He, despite his youth and the seemingly passionate advocacy of freedom for his client, took the dictate that she be further incarcerated for at least a fortnight, with all the disinterested aplomb of an 'old sweat'. She was followed in the dock by the fine defaulting Johnny Miller, who was – in the short term, at least – released but was guaranteed forty-two days in Exeter Prison should he fail, even once, to keep up his promised payment of ten pounds per week. The male members of the bench considered it an odds on bet that this feckless, indolent young man would be the guest of Her Majesty well within a month.

As to the turbulent Danny Durban, any further violence from him would be committed against prison officers or fellow inmates – most of whom would be more than a match for the slightly built young man who had ever puzzled the many magistrates in front of whom he had stood during a criminal career which had spanned ten years, he having begun as a fourteen year old youth. For it made little sense that a fellow not physically equipped for violence spent so much of his time committing it. Whatever, the young man was remanded in custody to Exeter Prison. His solicitor, Julian Higgins, made a bail application on his behalf, but did so with a total lack of both conviction and enthusiasm, merely going through the motions in accordance with his client's instructions.

He began his very brief verbal submission with the telling phrase, "My client instructs me to say," which from a hardened old pro like Higgins was tantamount to saying to the bench, 'You'll need your heads tested if you give this fellow bail'. Thus did the trio listen to the submission; the chairman then thanked Higgins, and, after a brief consultation with his colleagues, refused bail for Durban, even Molly Francis not raising any objection to his further incarceration.

Following the custody cases – which took a goodly amount of time – the bench began dealing with the rest of the day's list in brisk, businesslike fashion. Myriad motoring cases – the majority being postal pleas of guilty – were adjudicated swiftly, a couple of cases adjourned for the attendance of the defendants, as the points which were about to be added to their licences would take them to – or beyond – the fearsome twelve point mark, thus disqualification unless powerful mitigation could be produced.

The drink driver, Clive Partridge by name, still insisted on pleading not guilty despite Julian Higgins' advice to him that he enter an early guilty plea, and even after the solicitor's stark warning to him that if found guilty, the sentence would be harsher than if he had immediately admitted culpability. Indeed, there was a possibility now that the man, if convicted – as he almost certainly would be – would go to prison. The reason for such pig-headed stupidity from the accused man was not totally clear to the solicitor, but he suspected that the fact the fellow was about to go on holiday imminently – one which would involve him driving to Scotland, and around it, for a fortnight – was more than a little relevant. He suspected that upon his return, Partridge would change his plea to guilty, accept the inevitable long disqualification and hope that such a plea would keep him out of Exeter Prison. The solicitor had shrugged his shoulders – mentally at least – over the fellow's plea; after thirty years or so representing the dishonest, feckless, dissolute, violent, weak, foolish, inadequate and plain daft in local courtrooms, the actions of his clients had long since failed to worry or surprise him. It was, after all, just the day job, and it paid the bills – with a fair bit left over.

Max Burton glanced at his watch – ten minutes to one, and there was still work to be done, including jailing the fearsome Helen Harding, sat at the back of the court, a small attaché case beside her, poised and eager for her moment of glory, anticipating her martyrdom with relish, as, indeed, were the still largish numbers of journalists sitting waiting potentially for the story which would feature in newspapers nationally as well as locally. The magistrate felt a touch disappointed; he had things to do that afternoon, but he could see that probability suggested a good portion of that time would be spent in this courtroom.

Malcolm Naylor shuffled the papers laying before him, and

was about to get to his feet, when he was approached by the usher, Mrs Coleman, who gave him an envelope and a note written in her own hand. He thanked the usher in his courteous way, read the note, got slowly to his feet, turned and faced the bench.

Jack Dixon followed his colleague's example, and glanced at his watch. "I note it has gone ten minutes to one, Mr Naylor. Rather than starting another case now, it might possibly be better to just adjourn the court until two o'clock. After all, it's certain we'll have to come back."

The legal adviser shook his head. "I really don't think that will be necessary, sir," said he, "we have only two cases left, and it is unlikely they will occupy more than a few minutes of our time."

"Well – that's splendid," replied the chairman with enthusiasm. Like Max Burton, he had things to do that afternoon.

"Firstly, Your Worships, if we could deal with the charges against Sarah Douglas, charged with failing to keep under control a dangerous dog. The prosecutor leads me to believe he wishes to make an application."

James Sanders, an able, quite eager young man – who was expected to go far in his profession – arose swiftly, and gazed at the chairman. "Your learned legal adviser is correct sir. My application is to withdraw the charge against Ms Douglas regarding her dog. Unfortunately, yesterday the animal in question was the victim of a hit and run driver. Ms Douglas found its body in the road just outside her front gate. Naturally she was upset by this occurrence, and I feel it is in the interests of justice if the charge is withdrawn." The prosecutor made a slight bow, and sat down.

"I reckon the fellow who had the bite got his own back," muttered Max Burton in the general direction of the chairman.

Dixon smiled briefly, nodded his agreement with his colleague, then intoned, with some relief, "The case is withdrawn in accordance with your request, Mr Sanders."

"Thank you, sir," replied the young man, rising – a stickler for court etiquette despite his young years. Again he bowed, and sat down.

"Finally, Your Worships, we come to the case of Helen

Harding. Will you come to the front of the court, Mrs Harding, please."

Even the urbane legal adviser was a little taken aback by the alacrity with which she hastened from the back of court to the dock, a fierce and almost triumphant expression on her face, her case clutched in her right hand. Throughout her life, a lady of uncompromising and, at times, intolerant opinion, she was relishing her appearance in the dock this day, as would a Shakespearian actor taking the stage as Hamlet at the Old Vic. The regiment of journalists eagerly awaited developments, pens poised expectantly.

"You will be aware, Your Worships," said Naylor, turning and looking at the bench, "that Mrs Harding is in attendance today to either pay the seventy pounds which she owes to the district council, or to be committed to prison for twenty-one days. At the beginning of court this morning, nothing had been paid."

As Naylor stopped talking, and cleared his throat, pens began to move upon reporters notebooks, and the expression of triumph upon Helen Harding's face grew ever greater.

"However," the legal adviser continued, "I am pleased to say that during the morning our usher, Mrs Coleman, was approached by a person outside the court, who gave her an envelope containing seventy pounds cash, in full payment of Mrs Harding's debt. This money will, of course, be passed on to the treasurer's department at the district council. In consequence, Mrs Harding is free to leave the court."

The elderly firebrand was for several seconds, totally speechless – an expression of rage turning her complexion a deepish shade of purple. Eventually she found her voice; "This, this, this is outrageous – I know nothing about this; I've given nobody permission to pay this. How dare they – it's, it's, it's infringing my civil rights. I refuse to accept it – totally; I don't want it – not a penny of it; give it back to the fool who left it and tell them to mind their own business."

"That's impossible, Mrs Harding," replied Naylor in his even way. "For one thing, the donor was anonymous – but even if we did know, we would not be able to give it back. For the only interest the court has is that the money be paid. Thus we have to accept money no matter what its source – as long as it is legal, of course," he added drily. "So as far as the court is concerned, seventy pounds was owed – and has now been paid. That is the end of the matter." As he said the words, he saw assorted journalists put down their pens with no small measure of disgust and prepare to leave the court storyless, whilst Helen Harding once more started to build herself up for a further tirade. "That completes your list, Your Worships," stated he with unusual haste.

Jack Dixon, taking a cue from the legal adviser, promptly stood up, to be followed by his two colleagues, rasped a rapid, "Bench will retire – good morning," and hastened, along with Burton and Molly Francis, through the open doorway into the retiring room, hearing a fresh volley from the highly irate council tax rebel as the door closed behind them.

"Thank heaven for that," cried Molly. "I'm so relieved – it would have been dreadful had we been forced to send her to prison. The thought of doing that has upset my entire morning. Oh, I'm so, so, so relieved." With that, she picked up her handbag, wished her colleagues a brisk, "Goodbye," and was rapidly through the door on the far side of the room and clattering down the granite steps.

"Well," said Max Burton with a smile, "the one and only Molly's happy about the outcome, even if Mrs Harding isn't."

"Yes – absolutely. Still it's good news and no mistake." Jack Dixon suddenly pointed towards the coffee percolator; "It looks like there's still enough left for a couple of cups – fancy one?"

"Yes, a quick one before I go. And a couple of those biscuits wouldn't go amiss either. Wonderful woman, Alison Coleman – gets nothing but the best biscuits for us."

The chairman poured out two full cups, passed over a much depleted plate of biscuits, and then sat down opposite his colleague at the table. He devoured one, covered in chunky chocolate, and downed a goodly part of his coffee, before glancing the way of his colleague. "Well, that was a good outcome I fancy. The press people weren't impressed, mind you – they waited patiently for three hours – most of them, anyway, then ended up with no story. They must be savage. Just shows though, you never know what's going to happen in this game. Who'd have thought the money was going to be paid? No, you just never know."

Max Burton laughed. "Well, Molly certainly didn't know – and nor did I, if I'm honest. But the more I think of it I'm convinced that you knew only too well that was going to happen."

Dixon exuded an air of surprise. "Me – what do you mean? How could I know?"

"Simply because you made it happen, Jack – the district council have now balanced their books thanks to a seventy pound donation from you. I'm right aren't I?" A smile still played around his lips, but his gaze, riveted to the chairman's face, was unyielding.

"Why should I know?" protested he.

"Because half way through the morning I happened to glance to my left and out of the window, and who should I see coming towards the court, but your Sandy – and in her hand she was holding a white envelope. I thought no more about it at the time, but later – about half an hour before Mrs Harding's case was called, Alison Coleman came in and gave the clerk a note and a white envelope similar in size to the one Sandy was carrying. Even then the penny didn't drop, but when Naylor said the fine had been paid, I put two and two together and made – four, I fancy."

Jack Dixon laughed loud and long. "You've got it in one, Max – but I think it's best if we keep it as our secret. After all, I don't want to make a habit of paying other people's debts."

"Fair enough," agreed Burton. "But what made you pay it in the first place. I mean it would probably have done that old troublemaker a power of good to have to serve three weeks in jail. I bet she wouldn't be keen a second time."

"Don't you think so? I fancy the opposite is true. She'd have lapped up every moment of it. She'd have achieved exactly what she wanted – she'd have been a martyr. The papers – even TV news and such like – would have been full of it; and when she'd come out, I bet she'd have sold her story to a Sunday paper or some such thing as we said earlier. And us – we three magistrates? We'd have been painted as black-hearted villains; the media would have camped on our doorsteps – poor old Molly would have had a nervous breakdown. It might not have been too bad for you – after all you're not married and you work out of town a fair bit. But it would have played up hell with Sandy and me – and would have done our business no good at all. It's hard enough as it is running a business in competition with the supermarkets and multiples – this could have bankrupted us, literally. Dealing with the biggest villains in Devon wouldn't bother me in the slightest – but making a martyr of somebody, well, that was to be avoided if at all possible. Those were the lines my mind was running along when Naylor was going through the list before the court. I realised that if the money was paid, then that blasted woman would be sleeping in her own bed for the next three weeks, not in a prison one. So I went outside as you'll remember, and phoned Sandy. When I outlined the situation and made the suggestion that possibly a way forward was to pay the seventy pounds, she agreed totally and said she'd take seventy pounds cash out of the till, and drop it around during the morning. So that's what happened."

"Well, I see your point," conceded Max, "but it's still cost you seventy quid, Jack."

The chairman drank the remains of his coffee, stood up, put a couple of biscuits in his pocket as was his custom – "For the road," he would often say – then looked at his companion, himself preparing to leave.

"Max," said he, "if I live for another fifty years, I'll never spend seventy pounds more wisely than that."

# V

# The Lion in His Path

Arthur Burton gazed forlornly at his haggard reflection in the mirror, and slowly began to put on his tie. He noticed, vaguely, that the tie did not go with his shirt, but dismissed it as being of no relevance. Nothing seemed of any great importance to him at that moment; for this coming evening promised to bring one of the worst episodes of his life. Perhaps he should be putting a noose around his neck rather than a tie, he mused, as he completed the tidy knot in the flame coloured abomination which hung hideously down the front of his greenish shirt.

For this was the night when a vital part of his life would end; and it was all his own fault. If only he had not lost his temper. But then, that had been the story of his life. That wicked, white hot rage of his had always been more enemy to him than any mortal man. "It'll be the lion in your path," his mother had said, succinctly, when he was but a boy in short trousers, and few words had been more prophetic. And it was a beast which was now about to devour him.

Yet, it was not as if he were an unpleasant fellow; just the opposite, in fact. For he was basically an amiable man and had far more friends than enemies in the world in general, and in this old town of his birth in particular. Yet he could rage virtually uncontrollably, and on the very occasion when self discipline and a cool head were vital – almost invariably reaping a bitter harvest in consequence.

His last sowing of the seeds of his own destruction had been exactly one week earlier when he had exploded like a grenade, and, thus, had made a threat which ensured that his Janet had scarcely spoken to him since, would ensure that she would treat him with angry contempt for a long while to come, and would, this evening, make him appear a failure and a fool in the eyes of almost the entire town. If only he could take the words back – if only. It was all too late now, though. He had called up the devil within him and on this mild, late winter evening, Old Nick would be galloping in to claim his prize – the council seat, and high local standing of Councillor Arthur Burton, Deputy Mayor.

He reached into the wardrobe, took out the jacket of his suit and slipped it on. Then he opened a drawer next to the bed and took out a smallish, red case from within. The stiff catch giving way to his insistent thumb, he reached inside and removed its sole contents – a largish medallion on the end of a looped purple ribbon. He gazed at it wistfully, this outward mark of his position as Deputy Mayor of the town.

He could hardly bear to think how much he had wanted this over the years – and, of course, the major prize which would have been his, by the rule of tradition, this coming May – and of how, after this coming evening, this modest symbol of office would no longer be his; worse still, nor would the office that went with it. For tonight he would be forced to resign from the town council after fifteen years unbroken service. And, of course, if he was not a member of the council then he could not continue to be this year's Deputy Mayor – nor far more importantly next year's Mayor.

It was little wonder that he had incurred Janet's wrath to a greater degree than anything he had experienced in their twenty-six years of marriage. For she had coveted the position of Mayoress even more than he had wanted the principal role of Mayor. Not that Janet was pushy. Just the opposite, in fact. She was usually one of those people who would rather stay in the background, even though she enjoyed the involvement.

She had, however, been delighted when he had been elected deputy last May. For one thing, she felt it was long overdue – as indeed it was; he was easily the longest serving councillor who had never been given the chain. Also, although she realised that the beaming of the occasional spotlight upon her for that year, and the constant one during the mayoral term, would be both a strain and worry to her, it was something she felt that she ought to do for her own satisfaction and self esteem.

That had been very much in her mind when Billy Glanville, the incoming Mayor, had suggested that he, Arthur, stand for the Deputy Mayorship; but equally as important was the fact that if he had refused, Alan Plummer would have got it. Not that she had anything against Alan; the trouble was he was married to Doreen, a somewhat arrogant, opinionated woman who had deliberately embarrassed Janet at a council junket some five years earlier, and had thereby earned her undying enmity. Not a woman to easily forgive and forget, Janet.

Arthur Burton shook his head sadly – he knew he was about to incur his wife's wrath. Knowing Janet he was only too well aware that she would not forgive him for years – if ever. And, for sure, she had cause. If only he had kept his temper; but then, in fairness to himself, it was enough to make anybody of any sense or conscience blow a fuse. He closed the bedroom door behind him, went downstairs to the hallway, then into the kitchen and out into the porch. He put on his shoes without bothering to clean them.

After he had done what he had to tonight, the local papers would have a better story than merely to note that the Deputy Mayor was wearing grubby shoes, rather, they would be following up their previous week's story and telling all and sundry that Arthur Burton had tendered his resignation from the council and was, in consequence, the ex-Deputy Mayor with, no doubt, Alan Plummer – and his dreadful wife – filling the void.

He went out the back door of the house, got into his car, started it up, drove out into the road and pointed it in the general direction of the centre of the old Devon town – and the council offices. He felt like he was going to the gallows.

If only he could go back a week and start all over again. It was that blasted swimming pool, of course – as always. That monstrosity had bled the council dry for years. In fact, money went into it seemingly faster than water flowed out through the cracks at the bottom.

He had spent virtually his entire council service in opposing expenditure on it – with a singular lack of success. In fact, he had often proposed the closure of the pool altogether – without ever getting a 'seconder'. It was as if the majority of the council were terrified of making any decisions regarding the pool except that whatever amounts of ratepayers' money that needed spending to prolong its useless life, was spent. Granted, it was deemed popular amongst the public; or, to be more accurate, a number of folk had always written into the *Mercury* demanding that it be kept open every time he had sought its closure in the past.

Yet, he still believed that the 'silent majority' would rather have the pool closed and the money saved spent on something more worthwhile. Which is what he had said, forcibly, at the meeting of the Finance Committee the previous Tuesday evening. And he had stated, even more strongly, that he was totally opposed to the expenditure of £16,000 – agreed unanimously by the Properties Committee – on the refurbishment of the pool changing rooms.

"A complete waste of ratepayers' money," he had bellowed angrily, and added, "why, it was only refurbished a couple of years ago," with total accuracy. And had not Douglas Rogers spoken, then that would have been that; he would have contented himself by merely voting against it. But Rogers had instantly jumped to his feet and verbally attacked the Deputy Mayor – which was par for the course. For they had been at each others throats for years – ever since the time they had fallen out over a small business deal.

Rogers' attack took the form of a frontal assault in which he had accused him of constant small-mindedness and a perverted desire to take away one of the town's most cherished and popular amenities.

The words had stung him like a swarm of bees and before he had had time to consider his reply, his temper had exploded. He had jumped to this feet, his face the colour of liver, the words pouring from his mouth in a torrent. Much did he say – or, rather, shout – at the meeting in general, and at Douglas Rogers in particular, but the words which had caused him a week of sleepless nights since, and would, this evening, bring about his total downfall, in council terms, were the ones which terminated his tirade. Shaking his fist at Rogers he had said the fateful sentence; "This is the most stupid, disgraceful waste of money I've ever known in fifteen years on this council and I say here and now, that if this committee agrees to it tonight, and the full council next week, then I shall immediately resign from the council."

The words had no sooner left his lips than his mind had been gripped by the sheer horror of what he had said. Indeed, if he had not realised he had delivered an 'oral suicide note', then a glance at the stunned expression upon the face of his best friend on the council, Billy Glanville, would most certainly have told him. For the Mayor knew that the Properties Committee were unanimous for the spending of the money, and that the Finance Committee would be likewise – except for the deputy, of course. The first citizen of the town had not the slightest doubt that his deputy had put his head into a noose of his own making and that the stool would be kicked away at the full council when the decision to spend on the pool was sure to be ratified.

Arthur Burton steered his car into the council car park, finding a space by the far wall. He turned off the ignition, then sat still, gazing straight in front. So this was it – the night when his bluff was going to be called. He could, of course, keep his head down and conveniently forget that he had threatened to resign. He would be the only one in town who would forget it, though, the headline news in the *Mercury* that past week had ensured that. So, if he failed to stand by his pledge to resign, then he would lose all credibility in the town and his continued membership of the council would be rendered a charade. At least he would go out now with a modicum of honour.

He waited in his car, glancing occasionally at his watch. He did not want to get into the chamber a second before he needed to. He had managed to avoid contact with just about everybody for the past week and that was how he wished it to remain until he had done what he had to do. He had been fortunate his business as a sales agent had taken him out of town for a few days, so it had been reasonably easy to avoid phone calls and visits from the press, and from townsfolk and councillors who would either want to gloat, or give advice which would be of no help at all. He knew what he had to do this night, he knew there was no way out of it, and he wished merely to be left alone to handle it in his own way.

He glanced again at his watch. Three minutes to seven. Time he was off. He picked up the fat brown envelope containing agenda and minutes, got out of the car, locked it, walked through the entrance of the council offices, and strode purposefully towards the side door leading to the chamber. Without slackening pace, he entered, then made for his customary seat on the far side. He looked neither to right nor left, and spoke to nobody, lest a glance or a word betray the deeply emotional state he was in.

No sooner had he sat down, than he was on his feet again as the Mayor entered, with the town clerk, Henry Carter, at his side. Taking his place before the mayoral seat, Billy Glanville called the meeting to order, then proceeded with prayers. In accordance with time honoured council procedure, prayers were followed by apologies for absence, the signing of the minutes of the last meeting, any business arising, and then reports of the Standing Committees – and the first of those was Finance.

Edward Rolfe, the chairman, stood up and began to present them, minute by minute. Never a man to waste time, Rolfe fairly galloped through them, and the Deputy Mayor saw the fateful minute, number seventeen, approach like an express train.

"Number fifteen, grant to Boy Scouts," droned Royle, "number sixteen, review of salaries of manual staff; number seventeen, expenditure on refurbishment at swimming pool . . ."

Burton opened his mouth to speak, whilst getting to his feet, but was stilled by words from the Mayor.

"Regarding number seventeen, the town clerk has some information for us."

"Yes, thank you, Mr Mayor," said Carter, in his squeaky voice. "The fact is, I've had the district auditor, Mr Pollard, on to me about our spending this money on refurbishment at the pool. He read about it in the press, apparently, and is rather concerned. He points out that we spent a large sum on a similar scheme up there just a couple of years ago and feels that he might well have to take action against us if we spend more in the foreseeable future. This is a warning we would be ill advised to ignore, Mr Mayor, so I would respectfully suggest that we do not proceed with the scheme at present."

His words were met with dissent from the majority of the council, who did not take kindly to district auditors interfering directly in their affairs. The Mayor, though, was a past master at quelling this kind of outrage, and within a few minutes had calmed fevered brows and had gained unanimous agreement that the refurbishment of the pool changing rooms should be delayed for a year or two, when, as he put it, the district auditor's attention would be on something else.

Arthur Burton, for his part, just sat staring straight ahead like a zombie – but a happy one, for sure. For the realisation was slowly creeping over him that he had been saved. It was almost like divine intervention – though he had not seen the district auditor in that light before. Never, surely, had an evening begun so badly and ended so well. He would be Mayor come May, Janet would be Mayoress – and she would start speaking to him again.

He was still sitting in his chair letting the relief and pleasure wash over him, when he was summoned back into the world once more. "You're still one of us, then, Arthur," said Billy Glanville, standing in front of him. The deputy awoke, abruptly, from his reverie and, glancing about himself, realised only he and the Mayor remained in the chamber.

He nodded, "Yes, thank heavens, Billy. As long as I live, I'll give thanks for the district auditor."

Glanville laughed. "Yes, useful men district auditors, Arthur – especially when you know them."

"You know him?"

"Yes – know him well. Went to school with him. More than that, I was best man at his wedding. I knew that if I had a personal chat with him he would urge caution on the council. After all, that's the main purpose of auditors isn't it – to discourage councils from spending money."

"You mean – you brought him in on this?"

"No, not really. I just drew his attention to the fact that we were going to spend a lot of money we haven't really got on the pool again. I had a feeling he would react the way he did. I tried to phone to tell you, but you were away."

"Billy – I don't know what to say. I'm that grateful, words fail me."

"No need to feel grateful, Arthur. After all, we didn't want Alan Plummer to be the next Mayor, did we – not with a wife like he's got."

# VI

# The Show

Brendon Combe Flower Show was poorly named. For whilst there were indeed blooms of many hues and captivating fragrances to be seen and inhaled at the annual display, the event was actually dominated by the fruit and vegetable sections with the latter being the more important of the two. And of all the myriad classes which made up the vegetable section, the most prestigious to win (by common consent) was that given over to runner beans; no doubt largely due to the fact that this was the sole class in the entire show to have a challenge cup all of its own. It had been donated by the widow of a stalwart exhibitor of earlier decades, to whom the runner bean had been the king of all vegetables, and it bore his name: 'The Fernley Foster Memorial Cup.'

When she donated the trophy, Mrs Sarah Foster had added the intriguing rider – that anybody winning the cup four times in succession would keep it permanently. Now, over the forty-odd years of its existence several had won it twice in a row, a brace had gained it three times, but nobody had achieved victory on that elusive fourth consecutive occasion.

One of the pair who had done the 'hat-trick' was Bernard Clarke, a Brendon Combe man born and bred, who also held the record for having won the trophy on most occasions – eleven in all. The other was Martin Jenkins, a fellow who had moved into the village some five years earlier and who had won the Foster

Cup on the three consecutive occasions that he had entered his beans. So the show which loomed, just two days away now, would be his opportunity to put the trophy on his mantelpiece for keeps.

However, whether he deserved to do this was a very different matter. For whilst he was undeniably a good grower there were many in the village who claimed (with irrefutable accuracy) that the standard of runner bean which grew in his large garden, although being quite high, was well below that of the superb vegetables which regularly appeared on his show plate. And there were some who said, with perception, that his son – a prospering commercial gardener living some fifty miles away – invariably came to visit bearing a covered basket the evening before the show.

Now being one of nature' s gentlemen, Bernard Clarke did not mind in the least being beaten fairly, but he objected strongly to finishing second to a man who, apparently, cheated; and he thought that Jenkins could well cheat his way to the magic fourth victory in a row, and thus the winning of the cup outright. The very thought of it filled the local man with rage, an anger compounded by the fact that he knew he could do nothing to stop the fellow.

Certainly there was no way his beans could possibly beat those displayed by Martin Jenkins this year, even if the newcomer merely exhibited the produce grown by himself. For three weeks confined to bed suffering from a particularly virulent flu virus when he should have been out planting and nurturing his runners, meant that Bernard Clarke had rarely, if ever, grown beans of such poor quality and size. In fact, they were so bad that he seriously considered not entering any for the first time in almost half a century. His wife, Molly, however had other ideas and stated them bluntly to her husband when he spoke of his feelings that he should leave his undersized runners upon their plants.

"Not show!" she exclaimed. "Of course you must show! Jenkins has got to be stopped. Surely you're not going to sit back and let him swindle his way to winning the cup permanently?"

"There's nothing I can do to stop him," grumbled Bernard.

"You know the state of my runners this year."

"But there is: You can get some from Gordon. He's got some lovely beans down there, as you saw when we went there to dinner last Sunday."

Gordon was Molly's brother, an outstanding vegetable grower who lived in Plymouth and who had long dominated the vegetable sections of most of his local shows.

"I couldn't do that – it would be cheating," he rasped. "I'd be no better than Jenkins."

"You'd not be doing it for yourself, Bernard; you'd be doing it to stop Jenkins winning outright a cup which we all know he has no right to. It would be a service to the village as a whole."

Though Bernard Clarke was appalled by his wife's suggestion, when it came to a confrontation he was no match for Molly's quick brain and sharp tongue. Within half an hour he had been convinced that, in the interests of the integrity of Brendon Combe Show, he had to compromise his own by 'borrowing' some of Gordon's best beans and thereby, hopefully, stop the devious Martin Jenkins from gaining further rewards from his villainy. However, to appease his troubled conscience, Bernard told his wife that, as a penance for what he was doing, he would not enter his runners in the show the following year.

So the beans – specimens as magnificent as any Bernard had ever seen – were brought from Plymouth under a tea towel on the back seat of his car the day before the show and duly won first prize and the Foster Cup the following afternoon.

Normally Bernard Clarke would have been ecstatic, indeed it should have been the zenith of his long and distinguished association with the show and, in any other circumstances, he would have basked joyfully in the praise heaped upon him from the great number of folk delighted that the devious Jenkins had been prevented from winning the cup outright. This day, however, he made good his escape from the village hall as soon as he possibly could and, with the heart within him heavy with guilt, he trudged up the hill towards his home, absent-mindedly clutching the cup. He had rarely felt as depressed during his entire lifetime and he questioned what he had done. Yes, he had stopped Jenkins

– but at what cost to his personal integrity and honour.

He glanced to his side as he heard a car slow down and stop near him and a voice call his name:

"Mr Clarke . . ?"

"Yes, that's right."

"My name is Walker, Mr Clarke, Henry Walker," said the smartly dressed middle-aged man through the open side window of his motor. "I was one of the judges this afternoon, and have just stopped to congratulate you on your runner beans. In more than twenty years of judging I have never seen a finer collection. Magnificent – absolutely magnificent."

"Thank you," replied the gardener, tersely.

"Do you live nearby, Mr Clarke?"

"Yes; just at the top of the hill."

"Then perhaps I can give you a lift."

"Thank you," replied the cup winner once again, as he slowly got into the judge's car.

The motor moved off up the hill and was within fifty yards of its destination when the driver glanced at his passenger:

"I have to confess, Mr Clarke, that there is an ulterior motive in my driving you home. It's simply that the quality of your beans is such that I would really like to see where they were grown. I give a number of talks to gardening clubs and suchlike and would take pleasure in telling of how I looked around the exquisite garden of the man who grew the best runner beans I ever saw. You wouldn't mind showing me around would you?"

The gardener went a ghastly shade of grey and gazed straight and unseeingly ahead. Several seconds passed before he spoke, then he merely shrugged his shoulders in defeat and mumbled:

"No, not at all. You're very welcome. But it's only fair to point out that the beans I showed were, perhaps, just a touch better than any others I've grown this year."

# VII

# The Pit and the Pristine Machine

The mighty engine of Brendon Combe's new fire tender roared into life – eager to hurtle through the town to its first ever incident – as Frank Morton, officer in charge of the retained station, sped into the bleak, rainswept yard aboard his Ford Mondeo. He jumped from the car, ran into the station, grabbed his kit, threw it onto the appliance, followed it himself, and issued the terse command, "Get going."

The driver, Jimmy Windsor, did as he was bid, but as he guided the machine onto the road, quipped to his front seat companion, busily dressing into his firefighting gear – as were the four firefighters sitting behind them – "Unlike you to be the last aboard, Frank, especially as this 'shout' is the first in the new machine."

"I wouldn't have been if I'd been home," came the breathless retort. "As it was, I was a good two miles towards Plymouth on my way to Argyle. Damned nuisance this is; good game today – Wolves at home."

"I'd have thought the way Argyle are playing at the moment you're lucky you've got an excuse to miss it. Far better to spend an afternoon going out in our nice new shiny fire engine than watching them lose, isn't it?"

Morton did not answer; rather, he enquired, "Where are we going – what is it?"

"Moorlands Farm, out on the Okehampton Road," came the

voice of Vince Gregory from the back, who had been first to arrive at the station and had thus taken the emergency message. "Cow in a slurry pit," he added, almost as an afterthought.

"No," cried Morton. He momentarily held his helmeted head in his hands, then slumped back in his seat. "Stink, slime, muck, a blasted animal you can never get a rope around – I do hate these kind of jobs. And with a new appliance, new gear, new ropes; oh no. Why couldn't we have a simple false alarm or even a chimney fire, first time out?" he muttered to nobody in particular.

And his horror at the prospect of trying to rescue a large bovine from a vile pit was assuredly justified. For having arrived at the farm, then manoeuvred the appliance to the edge of the pit – a journey of some 100 yards across the filthiest of farmyards – he had only to cast the most cursory of glances to realise he had been given false information.

"That's no cow – that's a bull," he rasped.

The farmer, George Dalton, nodded in affirmation. "One of the best pure Devon bulls in the county," he said with pride. "I hope we can get him out all right; worth a lot of money, that animal."

"I bet he is," agreed the fire officer who, being a farmer's son, was fully aware of the value of such a beast. He drew his eyes away from the strangely subdued bull standing up to its neck in slurry in the narrow pit, and posed the question, "How did he fall in?"

The farmer shook his head sadly. "My fault; I should have had more sense. The fact is, I've recently bought a young bull – this one here's getting on a bit and you've got to look to the future. Well, the old fellow – Beefy we call him, for obvious reasons – is usually the most docile of animals, so we thought we'd put the new bull in the same field, as it would make life much easier if we could keep them together."

George Dalton shook his head again. "Old Beefy went maze – never seen him like it before. He chased that youngster around the field and would have killed him if he'd caught him. Well, the long and short of it is, the young lad was so terrified he smashed his way through the wooden gates at the far end of the yard, over there" – a slurry spattered finger pointed eastwards – "and ran towards the paddock on the other side. Beefy followed him – and skidded into the pit here." He shook his head again. "How we're going to get him out I really do not know."

Nor did Frank Morton – though he had more sense than to admit as much. However, the only thing to do at such times of uncertainty was to pursue activity. Thus did the Brendon Combe firecrew go to work, pulling ropes and straps from one locker, hydraulic lifting gear from another, even setting up a mobile pump should it be deemed a good idea to empty the slurry pit – a dreadful prospect.

After an hour, though, of slipping and sliding, getting plastered by the slurry, drenched by the incessant rain, freezing cold and increasingly depressed, the crew still gazed down upon the ever phlegmatic Beefy standing stoically in the pit. The fire chief called his men together and sought opinions as to the best way of extracting the massive bull from his putrid prison. The suggestions varied from the bizarre to the impossible, the over simplistic to the plain daft. During the debate Morton noticed a wizened old man, leaning heavily on a stick, shuffle up to the pit having come from the general direction of the farmhouse.

A man surely well into his eighties, he appeared to possess a keen eye and an air of shrewdness. After a brief chat with Dalton, the old fellow, accompanied by the farmer, shuffled up to the group. "My father's got an idea," said the younger man. He glanced at his elderly companion and, taking his cue, the old fellow spoke:

"George has told me what happened – and why. Now it seems to me that what got the bull into the pit is what'll get him out. He fell in chasing that youngster, so it could be that if the new bull is brought round for him to see, he could well get that mad he'll somehow scramble out to chase him again."

The idea was not without logic, and they were that desperate, anything was worth a go – though not one member of the firecrew thought it would work.

Thus George Dalton hastened off to the loose box where the newcomer had been put, and within a few minutes approached the slurry pit leading the animal by a halter around its muzzle and neck. Beefy's docility evaporated like mist in the morning sun. The mighty beast's head shot up, his breathing became heavy, there were snorts, to be followed by bellows – then total mayhem.

The animal dived and ploughed about the pit, slurry cascading everywhere, a goodly amount depositing itself upon both fire engine and crew. Suddenly with an unnerving roar, the hulking creature was emerging from the pit like a dolphin from the sea, albeit somewhat larger and infinitely dirtier and fouler. The farmer could see what was happening and rapidly pulled the young bull away – no great effort needed, for the animal was clearly terrified and scampered away behind his owner into the loose box. The farmer slammed the door shut just as Beefy, his sense of smell distorted by the slurry and his vision impaired likewise, went galloping by towards the nearby field.

Thus the emergency was over, and a slurry-ridden fire appliance – and crew – made a slow, smelly, thoroughly miserable return to Brendon Combe fire station upon completion of its maiden voyage. But the day's work was not done, for they were almost as long cleaning up as they were at the farm; thus all returned home in melancholy mood – and none more so than Frank Morton. For new fire appliances getting plastered in vile slurry he could come to terms with – his beloved Argyle losing was a very different matter.

# VIII

# Ginger and the Red Suit

It was not possible for the vast majority of the village to know if 'Ginger' Benton's nickname had ever been accurate. For the carrot coloured locks of his youth, which had validated the soubriquet, had gone well before middle age, and now, in old age, ceased to be a memory even to Maud, his wife.

"Bald as a badger, I am," he would trumpet; "have been since I was thirty." Losing his hair due to illness, though, like most of the other setbacks during his seventy-one years, had not suppressed a buoyant, genial spirit – even temporarily. Developments in the village during the past few days, however, had, and even his feisty wife found the lifting of his spirits beyond her. Not that she easily gave up on the task of trying to bring him back to normal.

"It's Christmas Eve, Ginger – time for you to snap out of this silly old sulk of yours," she snapped. "If you go on like this, you'll ruin the Christmas for me – and for Jim and Helen when they come for dinner tomorrow with the children."

Mention of his son, wife and family spurred the man to utter his first words for more than an hour. "I'll not ruin anything for anybody – and I'm not sulking. I'm just watching the film." His reply came in a tone of voice more sad than acerbic – and, in fairness, Maud knew that her husband had never been a man to sulk.

"Nonsense," she retorted. "When did you ever watch TV of an afternoon – especially Christmas Eve. You're just hiding away, aren't you? Keeping out of the way until six o'clock passes. I know you, Ginger – I can read you like a book, don't forget that."

"Well, what if I am? For over thirty years I've done it, and now they've just cast me aside like an old shoe; I still can't believe it."

"Nor can I, Ginger – but hiding away in here will solve nothing. Far better if you were out and about the village showing them you don't care."

"But I do care – that's the whole point. All those years at this time of a Christmas Eve I'd be dressing in my Father Christmas outfit and getting ready for the party. As you know, I did it for so long that when the old costume wore out they had a new one made especially to fit me. All those years – then they do this to me."

The 'they' were the organising committee of the annual Yuletide party for all children of the parish up to the age of ten, always held on Christmas Eve in the village hall, commencing at four o'clock. For the first few years, the Church Sunday School had run it but, because it had become so popular, many other village organisations and clubs had become involved, and the running of the party soon devolved down to a committee independent of all local organisations.

The format of the party had changed little over the years, though; the kids played games, had competitions, were entertained by clowns and so forth, given an enormous tea and then the highlight of the proceedings in the eyes of the children – and also the finale – they were each given a gift by Santa Claus. The first year of the event, Ginger had been Santa simply because he happened to be at the party – son Jim being one of the children invited – and donned the red robes and fluffy white beard when the fellow who was to perform the vital task failed to turn up. The next couple of years he continued in the job – Jim being still eligible by age, for the party – and then, being rather good at it, continued in the role when his son was too old to attend. And Ginger, being a good-natured outgoing kind of man, with a great affection for, and way with, children, enjoyed it. In fact, it had long since become one of the highlights of his year.

The previous Christmas, though, had seen him in very poor

form as Santa. The problem was that he had gone down with a mildish, though for a man of his age, rather debilitating bout of flu, just a few days before the party and though he was much improved by Christmas Eve, he was still not really well enough to don the red robes. Despite Maud's protestations, however, he dosed himself with aspirin – and a few Scotches – and went off to distribute the presents.

It had not, though, been the best of times for him. The combination of drugs and alcohol had produced unfortunate side-effects – such as slurred speech, confusion of the thought processes and a tendency to give children the wrong present. Aware that he had been in poor form, he had apologised to the chairman of the committee – Mrs Worth, a policeman's wife, who had lived but five years in the village – explained what the problem had been, and forgot all about it.

Sadly, the committee did not forget – though they took a very long time to react officially. Just three evenings previously there had been a knock at the door. When opened, it had revealed Mrs Worth standing on the doorstep, her long black hair tousled by the cold wind blowing strongly off Dartmoor. "Oh, Mr Benton," she had said briskly, "I'm sorry to call so late, but it concerns the giving out of the gifts at the Christmas party."

"Right – yes," replied Ginger, happily. "I thought I would have heard from you before now; still, no problem. Usual arrangements, no doubt. You'll have the outfit in the car, I expect."

"No – no, I haven't Mr Benton, I'm afraid." There was hesitancy, and embarrassment in her voice. "The fact is, Mr Benton, we held a meeting of the committee last night and decided it was wrong to impose on you any longer regarding the distribution of the presents. Last year you were – a little unwell – so we feel that it would not be fair to ask you to do it any more. However, we do thank you most – er – most warmly, for your past help; very greatly appreciated, Mr Benton. Well, I'll not keep you from your fireside any longer – goodnight." With that, she had turned on her heels leaving Ginger speechless as his eyes watched her disappear into the night.

And he had said little since – still bemused and deeply upset over the entire matter. The one thing of which he was certain was that his Christmas, if not ruined, held not its usual pleasure.

The film meandered on, as did the time, with five o'clock striking on the deep toned wall clock. The kids would be starting their tea about now, he mused, and at six they would receive their presents – but not from him.

He gazed unseeingly at the final reel of *Raiders of the Lost Ark* beaming out from the small screen and was so lost in his morose reverie that he scarcely noticed the insistent ringing of the front doorbell. Maud promptly left her chair, muttering standard phrases of annoyance, went out into the hall and opened the door.

"Mrs Worth – and what can I do for you?" Ginger heard her say – and in none too friendly a tone of voice. The redundant Santa, hearing mention of his name in reply, decided to investigate. He came into the hall and was suddenly greeted by Mrs Worth with an almost overwhelming effusiveness.

"Oh, Mr Benton, thank heavens you are at home," cried she. "I know it's ridiculously short notice, but could you come over to the hall and be our Father Christmas – as before?"

Ginger was rendered speechless – unlike Maud. "I thought you didn't want Ginger?" she rasped, belligerently. "I thought you'd got somebody else to do it?"

"Well – yes, we had; but – we've run into a problem I'm afraid," she stuttered. "The fact is that in about half an hour we shall have to give out the presents – and we've nobody to do it. So we – we – well, we were wondering if you, Mr Benton, would come around and do it for us, as in the past?"

Ginger's face registered joy, but before he could answer in the affirmative, his sharp-witted wife had interjected.

"Presumably you mean for the future as well – not just this year." The words were spoken more as statement than question – the tone aggressive, the eye fiery, the face taut. There could only be one answer and Mrs Worth gave it.

"Yes, naturally; we will be delighted for Mr Benton to be Santa at the party for as many years as he wishes," she replied – a sickly smile forcing itself across her face. "So – if you could come immediately we would be most grateful."

Within a few minutes Ginger had donned shoes, overcoat, scarf and hat and was sitting beside Mrs Worth as she sped through the village towards the hall. He glanced at her as she drove, then asked the question which was dominating his mind. "What went wrong, Mrs Worth – why did you need me after all?"

For a few seconds she said nothing; then, her eyes fixed on the road ahead, she replied – somewhat tersely – "The plain fact is that my husband was going to wear the robes. The trouble is he did not try them on until about an hour ago – when we realised we had problems. My husband is six feet two inches tall and sixteen stones in weight – and those robes were especially made for you, who are a great deal smaller."

"Five feet three and eight stone," he replied, chuckling. "No, there's no way they would fit – though that's something I never thought about these past few days."

"Nor us," she said. "And they wouldn't fit anybody else there, either. You are rather small, Mr Benton," she added, almost accusingly.

He smiled broadly as the village hall came into view. It was the first time he had ever found any advantage in being small; it seemed it was not going to be a bad Christmas after all.

# IX

# Christmas Story

Alan Forest dropped his cup heavily back onto its saucer, leant back in his chair, and considered the day ahead. It should have been a happy contemplation; after all, it was Christmas Eve and he had always loved the Yuletide season.

Yet his spirits were uncharacteristically low; for on this day he was almost certainly going to wreck a man's life – and it upset him just to think of such a thing.

Yet, what else could he do? For Jack Cooper had betrayed him – deliberately and systematically. He deserved no mercy.

Forest poured himself another cup of tea, and stared blankly ahead at the neat units which clung to the kitchen wall. He had been the only man in the town to give the fellow a second chance. Cooper had come to him in his office one cold morning with a sad tale to tell; not that he needed to impart it – the local community was well aware of his background.

Drink had long been the man's problem. It had broken up his marriage to a lovely girl, cut him off from his son and daughter, lost him a succession of jobs and, the ultimate calamity, condemned him to a prison cell.

For, drunk one night, he had clambered aboard his decrepit car, thundered through the town – and knocked down a fifteen-year-old lad on a crossing. The boy had died – and Cooper had served eighteen months in prison. Most of the town felt that the reprobate should have been locked away a great deal longer, but execution of justice and weight of public opinion are rarely compatible bedfellows.

Jack Cooper had, however, returned a seemingly changed man – for the better. The disciplines of prison had enabled him to overcome his drink problem, and put into him some semblance of desire to get his life in order.

So he had returned to his home town apparently determined to make a fresh start, and to surmount the natural resentment folk felt towards him. Thus, with that end in mind, he suffered, without retort, the abuse thrown regularly at him, and even refused to press charges against a bunch of local louts who had beaten him up.

So when he turned up at Alan Forest's builders' yard looking for a job on a November morning, the builder, a compassionate man, was inclined to give him one. For the ex-convict's call was well timed, Alan needing someone in the office. One of the two ladies who worked for him part-time had just left to have a baby, whilst the other was retiring early in the New Year.

He was strongly inclined to replace the two with one full-timer, for whilst it would cost him a little more in wages and National Insurance, and suchlike, the continuity provided by the same person being in the office on virtually every working day would be a considerable advantage. So, knowing that Cooper was a trained bookkeeper, and a man able to turn his hand to most office work, he offered him a job – an offer which was accepted with joy.

And for a couple of years it had appeared to be an inspired choice. Jack Cooper was highly competent in all that he did and Alan came to rely on him a great deal. And despite a recession in the construction industry, they had been quite reasonable years, business-wise, for Forest Construction, with the company more than holding its own.

Then, just the previous day, the auditor carrying out a routine check on the company's books, had given Alan shattering news. For more than £8,000 worth of company money had been embezzled during the previous two years, and, as he was in charge of keeping the books, Jack Cooper had to be the prime suspect.

Alan Forest felt he had no option but to call in the police, and as soon as he was confronted by them, the ex-convict confessed to the embezzlement, and was promptly hauled off to the local station.

So, on this Christmas Eve morning, Alan Forest was due at the police station to make a statement following which his employee would be formally charged.

The builder finished his breakfast, put on a heavy overcoat against the raw wind blowing down off Dartmoor, and walked out into the street . He considered driving down to the station but it was less than half a mile and it was a difficult place for parking at the best of times – and the Christmas Eve shopping mêlée was certainly not the best of times.

As he walked, his mind remained in turmoil over the matter – anger, incredulity, bewilderment, all flitting fleetingly across it. Jack was, seemingly, such a nice affable fellow. The builder had come to look upon him as a friend; yet all the time he had been misappropriating money – his money. Yet, as the police took him away, his face had mingled terror, panic and despair.

He had mumbled a pitiful, "Sorry, Alan – I really am; I meant no harm; it's just that I built up debts before I went to prison and I was desperate to pay them off. It was either that or lose my home. I've lost everything else, Alan – my wife, my kids, my prospects and my good name; I couldn't face losing my house as well."

With that he had been taken off to the station – but his words had hit their mark. For, despite his resentment at having his trust so betrayed, the compassionate side of the builder's nature began to assert itself. Would, he mused, anything useful be served by Jack Cooper going back to prison, as he most assuredly would after the case had come to trial. He would sack Cooper, naturally; there was obviously no way he could continue to employ a man whom it was impossible for him to trust. Yet, perhaps he would learn his lesson and take advantage of a fresh start somewhere else – as far away from the town as possible for everyone's sake.

Yet, if he could not trust the man, what right had he to expect someone else to do so. And, perhaps he would not change his ways – perhaps Cooper was essentially flawed. Perhaps he, Alan Forest, as a respected local businessman, would render service to the community by ensuring that this dishonest man was put away for a long while to come.

He walked slowly up some steps and entered the police station, stepping aside to allow a pretty teenage girl, her face awash with tears, to rush past him. PC Duncan, putting a notice up on the board just inside the front door, smiled as he saw the builder enter.

" 'Morning, Mr Forest. Reckon you've come to see the inspector."

"Yes . . . yes, that's right. Tell me, Constable, what was wrong with the young maid that ran out of here as I came in?"

"Oh, that was Jack Cooper's daughter, sir. Upset that her dad'll be off back to prison again. She doesn't live with him, mind you – hasn't for years, but he's still her father, I suppose." The constable returned to his task of pinning the notice to the board leaving Alan Forest to cogitate for a few seconds.

His task completed, Duncan turned to the builder. "Well, I reckon I'd better go and fetch the inspector so you can make your statement, Mr Forest."

The builder gazed at him for a couple of seconds then slowly shook his head. "No son – don't bother. I'll be making no statement on this matter, not today or any other time. In fact, I'll not be pressing charges. It seems to me that at Christmas there should be a bit of compassion in the world – a touch of goodwill to all men. I'll have to sack Jack Cooper, of course, but let that be an end to it. Let him go and have Christmas with his family – if they'll have him – and try to sort himself out again. Most important, let's see to it that that pretty little maid has a happy Christmas with nothing to weep over. 'Morning to you, Constable."

With that he spun on his heels and made for the door. Just as he was pushing it open, he turned and glanced back at PC Duncan who was looking somewhat nonplussed at the rapid turn of events.

"Good news for you son as well, isn't it really? I mean, the last thing you want on Christmas Eve is a mountain of paperwork."

With that final riposte he was out the door and into the street. He again pulled his coat tight about himself to help neutralise the snappy north-west wind, and turned for home. It was Christmas Day on the morrow and, suddenly, he was looking forward to it.

# X

# The Interview

George Barclay was bored. He was also fed up, disillusioned and thoroughly disenchanted with the world and the life which it forced him to live.

At his age life should be good. He should be approaching the top of whichever career tree he had chosen to climb, with income to match – and the prospect of retiring on a fat pension by the time he was fifty-five. Chance would be a fine thing. Here he was at the age of forty-eight not so much at the foot of the tree but rather lost in the middle of a barren plateau which appeared to have no trees at all. And at his age the chances of finding his sturdy, friendly, protecting oak were remote to say the very least.

He gazed about him and shook his head, the futility of it all overwhelming him once again. Indeed futility, like the tide washing over a beach, swamped him at least a couple of times every day. What was he doing here amongst all these young men?

The advertisement had read: 'Representative required for large sports goods manufacturers to cover Devon and Cornwall. Remuneration by way of attractive basic salary plus bonus. Company car, non-contributory pension scheme and other fringe benefits. Age twenty-five to fifty.' He had applied to the printed address as he had written to so very many others over the years – and had expected no reply. After all, usually the only time these companies ever wrote back was when they invited an applicant to an interview, and to reach that stage his name would have to be shortlisted.

Chances of that fell somewhere between the 'remote' and 'non-existent' range; had he not, after all, written for scores of jobs over the years, ranging from the good to the mundane, the interesting to the boring, only to have the vast majority of such requests for employment committed to some obscure waste bin in some overheated office. There had been the rare occasion, of course, when he'd been invited along to be interviewed by some idiot – or idiots – who would usually consider him totally unsuitable for the position for which he had applied; and there had been those so very few, even memorable times, when he had actually been offered jobs. Not that they had ever been much good. Usually treadmill, commission only, selling positions which were offered him because nobody else wanted them. Hard graft those when things were going well, soul destroying on those all too regular occasions when they were going badly.

He leant back in his chair and closed his eyes. How often he had tried to make sense of what had happened to his life. His childhood had been happy enough – though he had lacked aim, direction and a certain amount of discipline. After he left school these aspects of his character took control, overcoming a more than average intelligence and a shrewd view of life. He began to drift – from job to job, place to place (although he was never long away from his native West Country). When he met, then married Sally, he resolved to change, determined to beat out some decent future for them both, and for the children when they came along. In the early years of their shared life he was not totally unsuccessful. Being a man who had always, since young boyhood, been able to tell 'a good yarn', and who got on reasonably well with people – though he rarely got close to anybody – he had drifted into selling before his marriage, and was anchored there after it.

He was no mean salesman though, and could usually produce figures which were at worst adequate and at best excellent. The trouble was that a consistent personal selling ability and a progressive, successful company had never come together as far as he was concerned. If he'd done well then the company, overall, had done badly – one company had gone bankrupt and another into voluntary liquidation whilst he'd worked for them – whilst, for some inexplicable reason, he had never done well in personal sales when working for a successful organisation. Thus he had rarely worked long for such companies – and not at all for many years now.

He'd sold it all in his time – household goods, agricultural sundries, advertising space, clothing, insurance, even ice cream from a van one summer when nothing else was in the offing. But there had been too many jobs in the past ten years, each one, inevitably, a little less secure, a little less interesting, a little more pointless than the one before. For a couple of months now, he had been selling double glazing – occasionally. There was money in it, of course, if it was done well. There were two men working for the same firm making £1500 per week; the past month he'd not made a hundred pounds a week. He didn't really understand double glazing, not being a technical man; furthermore it wasn't a product he enjoyed selling. But then, if he were honest he couldn't think of anything for years he'd enjoyed peddling around. He'd like to try something totally different from selling – but was well aware it was far too late for that. He leant back on his hard backed chair and shook his head sadly; was it not far too late for him to enjoy any means of making a living? Would he be here at all – indeed, would he ever apply for any job of any kind – if Sarah was not there pushing him into it.

She seemed – in some outmoded way of thinking, to his mind – still to consider that it was a man's place to earn money to support his wife and children. Had she never heard of sex equality? Why should he be the one to earn a living? Why not her? A registered nurse, she was far more qualified to do so than he. Outmoded, unjust ideas, all of them. He'd worked for the first eighteen years of their married life, so why couldn't she be the breadwinner for the similar period of time which remained until they drew their pensions? The kids were both in their teens now – fast growing up and away. They would soon fly the nest, leaving their ageing, tired parents to live their own lives once again – as best they could. Certainly he had no ambition to carry on like he had been for so very long; he was jaded, and sick of it all. Sarah, though, did say, just a week or two previously, that when the children finally did go out into the world – or university – she would look for a part-time job in her profession.

"Mr Barclay, will you come in, please." A tall, immaculately dressed young fellow, not yet thirty years old, stood in the open doorway leading into the interview room and summoned him with courteous imperiousness, as indeed he'd summoned the four applicants who had already gone in to be vetted.

George Barclay walked into the large hotel room leaving the last two applicants behind him, and took in the familiar scene at a glance. Two men, both somewhat younger than himself, sat behind a huge metal desk and were quickly joined by the 'usher', who had rapidly closed the door behind the applicant and devoured the distance between doorway and desk with long, impatient strides.

Barclay sat himself down in the chair offered him, faced the trio and began, mechanically, to answer their questions. Strange, he mused to himself as he sent back the tired, hackneyed replies, how the questions never really varied. He had lost count of the number of times in his life he'd sat in chairs like this, in rooms like this, answering questions put by men like these (although they used to be older), and so very rarely had there been any point to it all. At the end of it they would thank him, and say that he would hear from them in due course; and that was true enough – a stereotyped letter would drop onto his front doormat within the next fortnight thanking him for his interest, wishing him all good fortune in the future, but regretting . . .

Still, to be in this room answering these questions at all was a mild triumph as far as he was concerned. The occasions of actually getting to the interview room in recent years had been few indeed. Obviously this was only a preliminary interview, of course, but he had been more than surprised when invited to it. After all, he'd only just scraped inside the upper age limit and, with his jaded work record of recent years, he was not exactly an exciting prospect. He had looked around him earlier in the afternoon before the first man had gone in for interview, and had been even more amazed that he'd been invited along. For there

were seven of them in the rather small room and he had to be at
least fifteen years older than the most elderly of the rest. It was
quite obvious they were looking for some keen, enthusiastic,
ambitious young fellow who could be moulded to the company's
image and sing the company song like a trained, caged canary.
And there would be a lot more after the job than just the seven
who crowded that room. This would most certainly be just a
preliminary chat with the slick gents in the big room; they would
probably have interviewed all that morning, yesterday, tomorrow
– perhaps an entire week; he'd known that happen before. Then
they would draw up a shortlist, upon which his name would not
appear, and start interviewing all over again.

As he answered some banal query from the young fellow who
had ushered him in, it suddenly occurred to him why he had been
asked along that afternoon. He was the token middle-aged
applicant – it was obvious now he thought of it. So as not to be
accused of any kind of age discrimination they had invited
applications from salesmen who were, by modern pressurised
business standards, almost in their dotage and had thus to
compound the charade by inviting one along for an interview.
Come to that he might not be the only one. There could well be
one a day for as long as the entire shoddy, absurd business lasted;
he just happened to be Wednesday's choice – 'Wednesday's child
is full of woe,' the irrelevant thought flitted through his brain as
he sat there hastily fending off the questions as would an aged and
failing tennis pro knock back balls to an enthusiastic, ambitious
young lad before the start of some third-rate tournament.

Yes, he felt full of woe, all right; this afternoon, like the bulk
of life itself, was but a waste of time. A thought came to him,
though, which brightened him just a little; perhaps they paid
expenses. Not all companies did, of course, but this was a
reasonably big firm so they might well do so. It wouldn't be a lot,
obviously, but even if it were only a tenner for the petrol then it
was better than the proverbial 'smack in the head'.

The questions meandered to a close, to be followed by some
information regarding the job. Standard stuff, once again – calling
on 'established outlets', and 'full back-up for the representative

from a large, progressive company' and so forth. Then salary was mentioned; "a starting salary of twenty-five thousand pounds per annum, to be reviewed yearly. Also there is a generous bonus scheme directly related to the representative's sales performance. On top of this there will be a company car . . ." The voice droned on but George Barclay was no longer listening. The first bit of information dominated his mind – twenty-five grand a year just for starters.

He couldn't believe it; never in his life had he been interviewed for a job with the kind of money they were offering here. Anybody landing this one – and holding on to it – was set up for life; with the bonus, car and other odds and ends, the job was worth at least thirty-five thousand a year. Suddenly he felt as flat as if he'd been knocked down by a steamroller. Why, after all, was he getting excited; he had about as much chance of getting this job as he had of being invited to become the Archbishop of Canterbury.

He sat there listening to them mithering on about their beloved company and silently cursed them. Why had they not left him in peace? Why had they invited him along that day? Far better if he'd never even had a reply – if he'd forever been in ignorance of the prizes there were on offer with this job. Within a minute or two this interview would end, they would thank him for coming, and tell him that they would get down to drawing up a shortlist once all the preliminary interviewing had taken place – and that he would hear from them in due course. And that, except for the letter of regrets which he would receive in due course, would be the end of the matter.

"Thank you, Mr Barclay, for your attendance this afternoon – and your candid replies to our questions," said the man sitting in the middle of the three, who was possibly the eldest of the trio and definitely the senior. "Seeing as you've nothing you wish to ask us, perhaps we can ask you to wait in the room through there –" he indicated a door to the right of where they sat; "and await our decision. We've only two more to interview, so we don't anticipate being a great deal longer. A good hour at most I would say."

George Barclay stared at him with no small measure of amazement on his face.

"You want me to wait?" he croaked.

"Yes, if you would, Mr Barclay. We expect to make an appointment to the position this afternoon."

"This afternoon?" he repeated, almost like an idiot. "You mean – this isn't a preliminary interview?"

"Good heavens, no, Mr Barclay. Yourself, and the other six gentlemen, comprise our shortlist. It might interest you to know that we had forty-seven applications for the position, and sifted through them until we came up with the seven most suited to the job – in our estimation. You seven are all here today and, unless anything unforeseeable happens, one of you will be offered the position before the afternoon is out. Not for us this protracted interview procedure, Mr Barclay – you know, where the successful applicant goes through half a dozen interviews over a period of weeks. A total waste of time, and company profits in our estimation. No, our decision will almost certainly be made this afternoon, so if you'd care to wait in the next room then you will be informed, along with the others, when we have made it."

"Thank you – thank you very much, indeed," he said quickly and almost enthusiastically. He pulled himself up from the chair and walked briskly from the room – some purpose in his stride now. He'd made a shortlist – and one for, possibly, the best paid job he had ever applied for. His chances of getting it were remote, of course – possibly nil; indeed, his place on that list was due, as he had convinced himself before, almost entirely to the fact that it was deemed correct to put the token middle-aged man on a shortlist, of that he was still certain. But it had done his confidence no harm at all, that was for sure.

The next hour and a half passed more slowly than any period of time he could remember. When he had entered that room and taken his place with the previous four interviewees, he had been pleased but the feeling was with him that he had no chance whatsoever of landing this excellent job so there was no purpose in worrying. As the minutes ticked away, though, he felt both expectation and hope rise within him. Why, he argued with himself, should his name be put on the shortlist if the company had no intention, from the start, of appointing him. The interviewers were busy men, surely far too busy to waste time talking to a 'token'. Perhaps, but then again . . . The arguments raged in his mind, the tension rose within him as the sixth man came out of the interview room and then, after what seemed an age, the seventh and last. George Barclay's nerves were as tight as violin strings; he pulled a handkerchief from his pocket and mopped up the sweat which beaded his forehead despite the coolness of the room.

His eyes became riveted to the clock face up on the wall, the red second hand moving on relentlessly. Would they never reach a decision? Once again he reached to his trouser pocket for his handkerchief – but his hand stopped by his hip; for the door leading from the interview room had opened and the young interviewer strode purposefully into the room, his tall frame transfixed by seven pairs of eyes. He glanced around him, obviously aware that he was very much the man of the moment.

He cleared his throat slowly, then addressed the far wall. "If you remaining gentlemen would stay for just a few moments more until I return," he said in a sepulchral tone of voice. Then he swept the faces with his gaze – and stopped when he reached the old man of the gathering. "Mr Barclay, will you come in again please."

George Barclay gazed at him for several seconds, his mind seemingly unable to absorb what was happening – then slowly nodded. "Of course; thank you," he said softly – but with a confident ring to his voice. He'd sold just about everything else – why not sports gear? And why, when all was said and done, should he not do it well? He knew Devon and Cornwall like the back of his hand; in fact, it was virtually impossible for anybody to know the counties better than him, having been born and bred there and having travelled its leafy meandering lanes ever since.

He rose from his seat without a glance to either side of himself, then strode purposefully behind the young man on the way to accepting his new position.

# XI

# The Tale of the Town Fields

"Alec – come here and look at this seat?"

The purposeful stride of Councillor Alec Conway was arrested in full flow; he knew the voice, and he was fully aware as to what the summons concerned. He glanced up and down the main street of the market town, virtually traffic free on this rather chilly May evening, and then crossed the road towards the tall, spare, elderly man who stood watching his approach.

The councillor was soon standing beside the ratepayer, Arthur Burdon by name, a reasonable enough fellow on the whole but, when it came to council matters, one with twice as many rights and complaints as any dozen other folks. He pointed accusingly at the sorry apology for a public bench squatting on rapidly rotting legs in an alcove of the low wall which divided the ancient, long since full, churchyard, from the pavement.

"How can you expect anybody to sit on that, Alec? Look at it, man. It's riddled with rot; in fact, one of the battens at the back is broken in half. You take your life in your hands sitting on that seat. It's time it was either repaired or replaced – as I've told you before."

Alec Conway shook his head, an expression of total mystification upon his face. "I'm sorry Arthur – I really am. It should have been done months ago; I can't understand why they haven't repaired it." Not exactly a true statement, that one, as the councillor was fully aware; for he knew that amongst the reasons why this well patronised seat had not been brought up to standard was simply that he had forgotten to report its deficiencies to the maintenance staff of Brendon Combe Town Council, despite being reminded by Arthur, and others, on at least three occasions.

"You leave it with me, Arthur – I'll raise cane about this."

"You said that last time," retorted the sorely disillusioned ratepayer.

"Yes – fair comment," replied Conway, hastily. "The trouble is that I'd just assumed something had been done. I've not walked along this way for a while; that's the trouble with a car, it takes away the use of your legs if you're not careful. My missus reckons I'd drive the car up to bed if the stairway was wide enough," he added, with absolute truthfulness.

"Well, as I said just now, it needs either repairing or replacing – with the latter being favourite, I fancy. With the state it's in, it'll be hard to repair. A new one – that's the best plan. It's used a lot, this seat is you know. 'Course, in fairness, it's not all wear and tear; a lot of it's vandalism. Some of these youngsters have got no respect for anything these days. Birch 'em I would. Why, when I was their age . . ."

"Yes, they're a menace and no mistake, Arthur," the councillor interjected with alacrity. He had heard Mr Burdon on the subject of corporal punishment before – at great length (though that diatribe was still briefer than the good man's monologue on hanging). "You leave it with me – I'll get hold of the works manager and bend his ear, don't you worry. I shall be seeing him tonight so I'll find out why nothing's been done and ensure something is." It was a promise with some substance this time, for Alec Conway did not want to alienate the old folk. Indeed, he had long since relied on the pensioners' vote – and it was principally senior citizens who sat on that seat.

"Anyway, Arthur, I must go – got a meeting in a few minutes." He moved away from the elderly complainant to the edge of the pavement in preparation for re-crossing the road.

"What meeting is it tonight then, Alec? It must be something important – you've got your best bib and tucker on, I see."

Arthur Burdon was quite correct – the councillor was smartly dressed indeed, which was not the most regular of occurrences, Conway being well known for a distinct lack of sartorial elegance, or even tidiness, much to the chagrin of his smart, attractive wife, Jill.

"Mayor making, tonight, Arthur; Malcolm Turner gives up the chain, and Myra Morrison will be wearing it for the next twelve months."

"How do you know it will be her?"

"Well, she's the Deputy Mayor, and it's custom for the deputy to be made up. It's always been the way – never known the deputy fail to become Mayor yet, and I've been on the council for nigh on twenty-five years."

"Don't like her," snapped Burdon. "Sort of woman who's got her nose into everything; sort of woman with ideas, and most of 'em daft – and expensive for the ratepayer. Bit of a lefty as well to my way to thinking – and one of them 'Women's lib' sort of women who's always on about the environment and so on, but keep their own garden, and house as well for that matter, looking like the corporation tip. No she won't be a good choice."

"Oh, she'll be all right, Arthur. Anyway, there's nothing she can do unless a majority of the council support her. She's only a figurehead, really – like the Queen – except she'll cost a fair bit less to keep in office during the next year."

"It'll all still cost too much, I fancy," retorted the old fellow, belligerently. "In fact, there's far too much public money squandered on you councillors. I mean tonight I bet there'll be liquor by the gallon and food by the skipful for you all – and all of it out of public funds."

"What?" snorted the councillor. "You must be joking." He laughed ironically, indeed, almost bitterly. "We'll be lucky to see a glass of sherry and a crisp each. And whatever we do get will be paid for by the Mayor herself – nothing from the public purse. Barren, belt tightening events these usually are, Arthur. Still, I really must be off or I shall be late – and that would never do. Take care." Raising his hand in farewell, he plunged across the street and turned the corner into the narrowish lane which led to the council offices.

He smiled to himself as he scurried along; he had heard all about these fantastic junkets enjoyed by local councillors but never seemed to be around when they actually took place. Nor, indeed, had anybody else on Brendon Combe Town Council as far as he was aware. Yet they obviously happened – Arthur Burdon said they did, and that was an end to it.

Mind you, the outgoing Mayor, Malcolm Turner, had taken office with style, producing half a dozen bottles of Scotch – as he had done some ten years or so previously when he had become Mayor the first time around. It was quite rare for anyone to be Mayor more than once, but Turner was an exceptionally able man – though undoubtedly an arrogant and self-opinionated one – and he had made a first class Mayor on both occasions.

He was also, being a dentist, comfortably off and able to put aside a lot of his own money, as well as time, to ensure that the wide ranging social side of the mayoralty was performed with both dedication and panache. That year was certainly the best Mayor making he could recall, for at least half the council said they did not like whisky and so stuck to sherry. He had not remembered much about that evening, but was regaled about his condition on arrival home – thanks to a lift from Councillor Ian Morton – by Jill the following morning. Not a good day, that one, confronted by an angry wife, whilst enduring the sort of headache which made death appear a soft option.

Still, it would not happen this year. Myra Morrison was the sort of woman who would provide only the barest of hospitality, preferring instead to spend money on the underprivileged of local society – worthy and noble, as Alec Conway would most certainly concede, but not really within the spirit of the event, in more ways than one.

Despite his 'seat inspection' with Arthur Burdon, Alec Conway was still in time for the beginning of the annual general meeting of the Brendon Combe Town Council. Burdon, though, had done him no small service by making him arrive at the meeting later than he would normally have been; thus he missed all the 'jockeying' for office which inevitably preceded the official gathering, the "I'll back you for Chairman of . . . if you'll back me for . . ." and so on.

Usually he would have had his support solicited by candidates for various chairmanships and offices of the council over the telephone during the evening or two preceding the AGM, but this year, mercifully as far as he was concerned, his job as a locally based agricultural representative had, most unusually, taken him away from the area for a few days on a sales course, thereby making him unobtainable to those who saw his support as being vital to the fulfilment of their ambitions. For, being a veteran in terms of council service, Alec had done virtually all of it – been Chairman of the Properties Committee, of the Finance and General Purpose Committee, Deputy Mayor and, the zenith of his civic career, Mayor of Brendon Combe – and had no ambition to do any of it ever again, an attitude well known amongst his fellow councillors. Thus, as he was in no way a rival, his support for their own ambitions was seen by all the 'upwardly mobile' as being vital.

It was a role which irritated him intensely; not ambitious for himself, he was not ambitious for anybody else, either. The role of 'king maker' held no appeal. There was a moment during the meeting, however, when he had wished that possibly he had taken some small part in trying to work out beforehand who should be Deputy Mayor to Myra Morrison for the ensuing year.

For no fewer than three candidates were proposed, none withdrew their nomination voluntarily, so the issue went forward to a vote which proved to be somewhat fractious. The triumph of Gerald Dunlop, who had only been a member of the council for two years, was received with bad grace by Anita Collinson, one of the defeated candidates, and provoked in Gordon Holland, the other vanquished hopeful, a threat to resign from the authority. "Seven years I've been on this council, Mr Mayor, and Mr Dunlop has been on a dog's watch. Yet he gets the deputy's job, and I don't. I fancy I'll get no justice from this council – I reckon it's time I considered resignation. It's a 'shake hand hang' effort here, I can see that."

This had brought Gerald Dunlop to his feet, almost apoplectic with rage – a fuse shorter than a wren's beak had long been the new deputy's Achilles heel.

"Mr Mayor, I protest. Whilst I am a Mason – and I make no apology for belonging to such a worthy, philanthropic organisation," he roared, his voice pregnant with belligerence, "my elevation to the Deputy Mayorship of this town owes nothing to that whatsoever – and Mr Holland knows that, if he is at all honest. Perhaps, Mr Mayor, he should look to himself and his own inadequacies as a councillor for his failure to gain this office. Perhaps . . ."

What Gerald Dunlop was about to say nobody would ever know, for the moment saw a finely judged intervention by one of Brendon Combe's finest councillors, Susan Matthews, amongst the longest serving members and a woman of immense judgement and integrity. Seeing Gordon Holland's face turn almost purple with rage, she had risen just before Dunlop was able to twist the knife in the wound he had already inflicted upon the defeated, and somewhat vulnerable candidate, and proposed simply and clearly to the meeting, in her customary straight-forward manner, that, "Mr Holland should be elected Vice Chairman of the Properties Committee for the ensuing year," assuming that she would, herself, remain as Chairman.

She had been in the chair for the past twelve months and it had long been custom that a chairman of a standing committee do two consecutive years, unless they had made a real 'pig's ear' of it. Susan Matthews never did anything, in terms of council work in any way that was other than excellent, so there was no doubt that she would occupy the chair for another year.

So, if she was happy to have Gordon as a vice chairman – to take the place of Henry Wilton who had died just three months earlier of a heart attack, and whose place on the council had been taken by Hilary Spencer, the youngest and unquestionably, to the male members, best looking woman to come onto the authority for many a long year – then it seemed a reasonable compromise. Certainly the resignation of Gordon Holland from the town council – and he was mule headed enough to do it, even though he would regret it immediately afterwards – was something to be avoided. Not that he was any major asset to the authority; he was too erratic of judgement and temperament for that. Rather, it was that with all the ever escalating costs and commitments coming the way of the council, they could ill afford to fund a by-election. There had already been two in only nine months – the one which elected Hilary Spencer, and one the previous autumn which had seen Fergus Allenson, a studious, quiet, but most perceptive man, a teacher at the local comprehensive, elected to take the place of Dennis Bailey, who had resigned saying he had more important things to do with his time, immediately after his wife had run off with a local insurance agent. The then Mayor, Malcolm Turner, amongst other things a man of acerbic, and, at times, quite cruel wit, had remarked after the meeting during which he had read out Bailey's letter of resignation, that it would appear now, that the departing councillor would have nobody to do the important things with during his spare time; but, as he so rightly said, "theirs not to reason why."

Gordon Holland accepted the vice chairmanship of the Properties Committee with reasonably good grace in all the circumstances, glad – though he would never admit it – that he had an excuse not to resign. He did, however, add the rider that whilst he was willing to accept the number two position in the Properties Committee, he would expect the council to acknowledge his loyal and sterling work for the local community by making him Deputy Mayor, and then Mayor, in due course; not a modest man, Gordon Holland.

No commitment was made by the council as to if or when such office would come his way, and the meeting rapidly moved onto 'next business', which was the speech of acceptance of office by the new Mayor, Myra Morrison. Such diatribes were usually sleep inducing, but Myra concentrated minds in a way few previous holders of her office had succeeded in doing. An intense sort of woman, an active member of CND, Friends of the Earth and a doughty champion of the under privileged – though not an overtly political person in the party sense – she appeared to see the town council as an active branch of the United Nations, committing herself, and she hoped, her colleagues on the council, to campaigning and fighting for everything from a prospering recycling policy to a ban on all new planning permissions, from vastly greater grants out of the public purse towards myriad charities in the town and those supporting aid and welfare for the Third World, to giving the use of the Town Hall, and all other relevant council owned property, free of charge to all 'worthy' organisations – worthy, no doubt, in Myra's eyes, though probably nobody else's.

As he sat listening to her long and impassioned speech, Alec Conway had an uneasy feeling that it would be necessary to keep 'an eye' on the new Mayor. In the midst of such thoughts, they were confirmed by a comment from Claude Partridge sitting next to him – though 'slumped' would be a better description. A semi-retired farmer nearing seventy, Claude was the 'father' of the council having been a member for some thirty-five years. He said little and did less, and always lay in his seat like a sack of potatoes. Yet he was a very perceptive man who had seen most if not all before, and had forgotten nothing.

Often, with a few profound words uttered from his sedentary position, he had solved seemingly intractable problems, settled internecine squabbles, chopped down to size those members whose ego exceeded their abilities and made predictions which were usually correct as now, when he stated simply, "She'll need close watching will this one; she'll cause this council no end of problems if we're not careful."

Alec Conway nodded his agreement, and returned his attention to the continuing rhetoric of the speech – which was not brief. It was not so long, however, that it was incapable of producing a sting in its tail. For as Myra Morrison replaced her notes onto the high desk before her, she uttered the words which concentrated minds more than anything else she, or anybody else, had said all evening.

"It has long been the custom fellow councillors, ladies and gentlemen," – addressing the thirty or so townsfolk who had come along as either invited guests of the incoming Mayor, or just to view the proceedings – "to offer sherry, wine, even, at times, spirits," (she spoke the word in a tone of condescending distaste) "to drink, with canapés and suchlike to eat. Today, however, to set the tone for my year of office which, as I said just now, is largely going to be dedicated to the disadvantaged in our society, I am providing only mineral water to drink, and nothing at all in the way of foodstuffs. The cost of this to myself will be considerably less than if I provided the traditional drinks and fare, naturally. So what I have done is to calculate how much money I have saved, and will shortly forward that amount to some selected local charities. I hope, ladies and gentlemen, that by doing this, I set an example which you will all feel able to follow. With that in mind, I have left a series of collecting plates at the back of the chamber for you to make what contributions you feel able towards local charities. Thank you all for your forbearance and attendance."

"I told you she'll need close watching," muttered Claude Partridge to Conway, as the new Mayor sat down to somewhat ungenerous applause. The post 'mayor making' reception was the briefest anyone connected with Brendon Combe Town Council could remember. Most councillors did exactly what Alec Conway did; he totally ignored the mineral water – "I'll not let stuff like that pass my lips," he said to Susan Matthews, who was womanfully sipping a wine glass full. "Not unless it's diluted with whisky," he added with a grin.

Susan smiled; "Yes, it is a little different from last year, isn't it?"

After ten minutes conversation with Susan and a couple of others present, he sought out Myra Morrison, congratulated her, wished her a successful year in office – a reality he doubted increasingly – then made for the door of the chamber, deliberately going via the poorly patronised collection at the back in order to display his disgust at the new Mayor's attempted coercion by walking past her 'begging bowls' and putting in not a single penny.

There was nothing the matter with charity, he mused to himself, but he would choose when, and to whom, he gave. And he suspected that Myra Morrison's idea of the deserving in society would encompass the eccentric rather than the deprived. Passing through the open door into the wide corridor which led to the street, Alec saw the short burly figure of Colin Butler the works manager making good his escape from the alcohol free proceedings. "Mr Butler," he called after the council official just about to make it to the street, "the Mayor wishes you to report to the town clerk in the morning with a statement, written in triplicate, as to why you've escaped early and have not consumed at least two pints of mineral water."

Butler swung around and saw the councillor approaching him, a wide grin on his face. The two were old friends of long standing, Alec Conway having been an elected member of the town council a mere twelve months longer than the works manager had been an official. Men of similar age and interests, both lifelong supporters of Plymouth Argyle, they had quickly established a rapport, Conway usually finding the direct approach to Colin Butler being the best, speediest, and most effective way of solving problems.

Thus if there was something concerning the town council's properties which needed repairing, inspected, sorting out, unless it was a major undertaking, Alec, along with some other councillors, tended to bypass the pedantic fussiness of the town clerk, Harold Newman – competent man though he generally was – and the nit-picking of the committees, and go direct to Colin. For his part, the works manager would often bring problems to Alec, or to the same small nucleus of elected members, knowing that, generally, they would be solved with a minimum of fuss, and in a mercifully short period of time.

"I've worked for this council a few years now, Alec," retorted the official as the councillor came up to him, "and another before this – long time back now, of course – but I've never known a Mayor making like that. And I've never known a speech like it, either – not that it's my place to make comment on either, mind you," he added hastily. One of Butler's great qualities as a council official was that whilst he in no way gave out an aura of subservience, he saw the elected councillors as being, unquestionably, in charge, and himself as being, ultimately, their hired servant.

"Less said the better, I fancy, Colin," replied the councillor, interested in talking of more important current matters. "What I wanted to ask you about is that broken seat."

"What broken seat?"

"The one sited in the wall around the church – you know, on the corner of Regency Street."

The works manager looked suitably vague.

"You know, Colin," persisted Conway, "the one opposite the Mothercare shop."

"Oh, that one; I'm with you now. Yes, it is in a bit of a state. Blasted vandals again."

"A bit of a state? That's an understatement if ever I heard one. And it's no good blaming vandals, either. Granted, they've probably played their part in its general deterioration, but the main problem with it is that it's rotten to the core and has been for years. Not like you to miss a thing like that, Colin," he admonished, gently. "You're usually on the ball when it comes to seats; in fact, the overall state of the public benches in the town is excellent."

"Well, basically it's in a bad state Alec, because it's not ours. If it had been I'd have got it sorted out long ago."

"What do you mean, not ours – I thought the town council owned all the seats in the town."

"We do – except for that one, and another on the far side of the wall; you'll know the one – the big wide seat that's sited opposite Woolworths; the one where all the local yobboes seem to congregate."

The councillor nodded. "I know the one; I wouldn't worry so much about this seat if it was mainly yobs that used it. Just the opposite with this one – it's mainly pensioners who perch themselves on it and I daren't upset them, Colin. I get half my votes from the old folk," he said with a grin – but also quite truthfully. He had, for reasons he never understood, always seemed to appeal to the senior citizens of the town.

"And of course, with the Mothercare shop being nearby, you get a fair number of pregnant women sitting on the seat as well. Imagine the hullabaloo if the damned thing collapsed under the weight of an expectant mother; my God, the council would be up in court, and the *Echo*" – referring to the local paper – "would have their best story for years."

"True enough," agreed the works manager, "but it wouldn't be the town council who'd be in court, it would be the district. They own that seat – and the other one I mentioned as far as I'm aware."

"Well, whoever owns it, it's time it was repaired – or replaced if necessary."

"Cost a few bob to replace it, Alec. Ridiculous price they are these days, seats."

"By the state of it, it'll cost a pretty penny to repair as well," retorted the councillor. "But something's got to be done – Arthur Burdon will have my guts if it isn't, and somebody else will have his vote," he mused, largely to himself.

"Well, leave it with me," replied Butler. "I'll phone the district council and get them to do something about it. Mind you, these days, with everything privatised and all that, it's no easy matter to get things done where they are involved."

"Why not?"

"Well, it's different up there than it is here as you know. With the town council, we control our own staff, small though it is. So if it was pointed out to me that there was a seat owned by us which needed repair, I'd merely tell one or two of the lads to go and attend to it. Simple as that. The district council though, technically, do not employ any maintenance staff now. At their level of local government, everything, as you well know, was put out to competitive tendering years ago, so there's a private firm that does all their maintenance, just as you'll be well aware, there's another that takes care of emptying the bins and yet another which does the street cleaning and such like. So even if the maintenance department at the district council agrees to do something about the seat, they do not have the power to send a couple of fellows to repair it – they have none to send, as I've just pointed out. They have got to get hold of their contractors, then go through the most ludicrously convoluted, time consuming, money wasting exercise imaginable just to get them to send a couple of their men to put the blasted seat right. It could take weeks, Alec, to be honest – perhaps months even."

The councillor shook his head in bewilderment. "And they call it progress," he rasped, his voice mingling frustration with despair. "Still, if that's the way it has to be, then so be it. As long as it gets done."

"Oh, it'll be done, Alec, don't you worry about that; even the district council do get things sorted within a tolerable period of time," replied the works manager with a confidence which experience should have told him was sorely tempting fate.

Just a couple of weeks after this, however, the councillor was given news which banished all thought of public seats from his head; for it concerned the Town Fields which were Brendon Combe's pride and joy. Some eight acres of open space; the land had been given by an aristocratic benefactor, into the keeping of the council well over a century before, was situated very close to the centre of town, and had something to offer for most folk, if not everybody.

The narrow river which ran through Brendon Combe divided the park, roughly, in half, with to the one side of it bowling and putting greens, tennis courts, even a croquet lawn, whilst on the other was the town swimming pool – the supreme loss maker amongst the many others run by the town council – a small cafe, the children's play area, a few flower beds, a small football pitch, and a couple of acres of lush, but well maintained grass, where people could, within reason, do exactly what they wanted.

So, at its best, the Fields were a tolerably idyllic spot; yet, during the evening following a pleasant early summer's day, Alec Conway was to be given news of a calamity which appeared to threaten the town's green paradise.

"Phone, Dad," called out Sally Conway to her father, who, after a hard day's work trying to sell to farmers was relaxing with Jill on the small patio in the back garden.

"Who is it?"

"Susan Matthews," came the reply.

"It's got to be council business," sighed Jill Conway, wearily.

"For certain," agreed her daughter.

"Oh no." The councillor slumped dispiritedly back into his chair. "There's never any peace, is there. Dammit, I've had a hard day, and I deserve a bit of peace and quiet."

"You choose to do it, Dad," retorted his daughter, twenty-one years of age, recently post graduate, due to start an executive job with a London publishing house in the autumn at a salary which her parents termed as ludicrously, though delightfully, high, certain of the direction she was going to take in this uncertain old world – and more than a match for her easy-going father. "Nobody makes you."

There was no argument to that, as Alec was well aware. Yet the odd bit of sympathy from his rather brash daughter would not come amiss. If Tom was at home now, he would have supported and sympathised with his old dad – whether he was right or not. Tom, though, was now a married man, and in six months would be a father, thus elevating Jill and himself to the status of grandparents – something they were both delighted about – and whilst he only lived the other side of town, his ever increasing hours dedicated to the successful establishment of a fairly new landscape gardening business, meant they saw far too little of him these days.

The councillor ambled into the house towards the tranquillity terminating little white monster squatting malevolently on a low table in the hallway, slumped down beside it and picked up the receiver.

"Evening, Susan; I trust you are well," he asked in his naturally courteous way.

"Physically, very well thank you, Alec," came the reply. "Mentally, though, I think I could be on the verge of a nervous breakdown – as, I'm afraid, you might well be when I've given you the news."

"This sounds grim," he replied, bracing himself for tidings which would, no doubt, ruin the evening; Susan Matthews was not the sort of woman to spread alarm gratuitously.

"It is grim, Alec. The fact is, we've got New Age Travellers camping in the Town Fields – on the football pitch."

"Oh no." The phone would never stop ringing when folk got to hear of this, he mused to himself. Still, it could be worse – they could be parked up on the bowling green.

"How many of them, Susan?"

"About a dozen, I think – and five vehicles. It could be worse, I suppose. I mean, there are so many of them in this area at present that we could have had twenty or more caravans and suchlike down there."

"That could still happen, couldn't it. This could just be the advance party. We've to get them moved on – and without delay. We'll have to get the police to take some action."

"I doubt they will."

"But they've got to," retorted Conway. "These people are trespassing – it's as simple as that."

"I'm afraid it's not, Alec," replied the Chairman of Properties in her soft but authoritative way. "The police usually can do nothing without a court order. And in this instance there is absolutely no chance of getting that."

"Why not, for heaven's sake?" he rasped; the woman was talking around the subject, which was not her usual style.

"Because they have got official permission to be there. Indeed, they were invited to camp in the Town Fields."

"You're joking, Susan – you have to be."

"I'm afraid not. These people were being moved off a wide verge a few miles up the road by police and the county council officials this morning, when who should come along in the middle of the inevitable altercation, but our own Town Mayor, Myra Morrison. And, being her, she took the part of the Travellers and when they wailed they had nowhere to go, she invited them to camp in the Town Fields for the time being."

"Susan, in all the years I've been on the council, this is probably the most lunatic thing I've heard. Are you sure it's true?"

"It's true all right – there's no doubt about that. Let me take you through it. I heard about it just under an hour ago – from Harold Newman. Somebody living opposite the Fields had seen the Travellers going in there and immediately phoned him as town clerk, at home, as it was past office hours, of course. Harold panicked – as he always does – and promptly phoned me as Chairman of Properties, desperate, naturally, to offload the responsibility onto somebody else. I thought about phoning the police there and then, but thought it only right that the Mayor, as the town's leading citizen, should be informed. So I phoned Myra, and was blandly given the news that she knew the Travellers were in the Town Fields because she gave them permission to go there."

"What did you say to her?"

"I shudder over what I said – with hindsight; though, in fairness, I said nothing she didn't deserve, and if I could rerun the episode, I'd not change a word. Basically, I spoke in deep anger and gave her a piece of my mind. I told her it was an act of irresponsibility that almost beggared belief; I told her that she was a disgrace to the people she represented, to the council itself, and brought the office of Mayor into total disrepute. In fact, I went so far as to say I thought she should take the only honourable course left open to her and resign."

"And what did she say to that?" An involved Alec Conway found this story to be compulsive listening.

"Oh, she said there was no way she was ever going to resign. She couldn't see she had done anything wrong. It was, in her estimation, an act of basic human compassion and she would do it again. Anyway, she said, the Travellers had promised her they would only stay two or three days."

"What? My God, if she believes that, then she must still believe in Father Christmas. It could be two or three months before we get rid of them – probably longer than that. It's hard enough to get court orders, and the police, to move them on when they camp somewhere without permission. But they've gone onto council property, technically, quite legitimately; what judge is going to grant us an injunction to have them removed when the first citizen of the town gave them permission to be there in the first place. The reality is, they could still be there in twelve months' time."

"I'm sure you're right, Alec. Still, there's nothing we can do about it in any way tonight. As it happens, of course, we've a meeting of the Properties Committee tomorrow evening, so we can chew it over then."

"As we will at great length, no doubt. Not that we'll come to any decisions as to what to do about it. I mean, we're rarely able to decide on a course of action when the problem before us is relatively simple. When it's as complex as this one, then we've no chance. Still, Myra Morrison will be there; she got us into this, so I reckon the committee must spell it out to her that we expect her to get us out of it."

"She won't be there – she gave me her apologies over the phone. She has got a Mayoral engagement. It's the Old Folk's Reading Room Annual General Meeting, and as you know, the Mayor is automatically their President for the year, and traditionally takes the chair. With the hornets nest she's stirred up due to swarm all over her if she enters the council chamber," the Chairman of the Properties Committee opined, lyrically, "I fancy it's one time when Myra will be very relieved to maintain tradition, and take advantage of a legitimate excuse to be as far away from the chamber as possible, for as long as possible."

"Yes – you're about right there."

"So I'll see you tomorrow night, Alec. And I would appreciate it if you could come up with some ideas as to a way forward in this. The reason I've phoned you first amongst the council – except for Myra, of course – is because you are one of the very senior members in terms of service, and also you're rarely short of ideas. Also – and I think this is important – you are the only member of the council who is also a magistrate. With that in mind, perhaps you could have a word with the local magistrates' clerk – obviously you'll know him quite well – and perhaps see if he has any views as to how we can approach this thing. Professional people like him know all the loopholes, so a bit of advice, or a few tips from him, could prove invaluable. And for sure, we have got to do something. If we don't, there'll be all hell let loose with the ratepayers. In fact, I expect our phones will be ringing a few times before this evening is out, when news gets around; it can only get worse."

"I'm sure you're right. And when folk phone, I shall tell them the facts – and point the finger in the direction of the woman responsible. I'm a firm believer in collective responsibility when

121

f

the council makes a decision – even when I might not agree with that decision. But the council's not had any say in this at all. The Mayor gave permission without a word to anybody else, so she can take the flak – and there'll be more of that than there is in the Middle East."

"I agree entirely, Alec. Anyway, thank you for listening to me. I'll see you tomorrow evening. Goodnight."

"Night, Susan – I won't say 'sweet dreams'. The best we can both hope for is no nightmares."

With that he replaced the receiver and leant back in his phone side chair. It was certainly about to 'hit the fan', as the saying went. And his phone shortly would most definitely be buzzing with all the insistence and continuity of angry bees; but then, as his Sally had said only ten minutes earlier: "You choose to do it."

Susan Matthews' comment concerning his position as a magistrate in the town was also relevant – and something which would not have occurred to him if she had not mentioned it. Not that the office gave him any direct influence over matters – on the relatively rare occasions when council affairs had directly come the way of the local magistrate's court, during the fourteen years he had been sitting on the Brendon Combe Bench, he had had to declare an interest and, accordingly, not sat on the cases, but as Susan had intimated, being a JP did give him the kind of informal access to the trained legal clerks of the system, most of them qualified solicitors in their own right, which would be beyond the direct reach of the other members of the council. He would most definitely contact the local chief clerk the following morning and see exactly where the council stood in legal terms. With the Mayor having given permission for the Travellers to camp in the Town Fields, he suspected that the authority stood up to their collective necks in deep trouble.

As for Alec Conway himself, he was to stand – or, after a while, sit – for most of the evening answering the telephone, and trying to placate angry residents over the matter of the 'not technically' trespassing New Age Travellers. Always a man to take responsibility for those things for which he was directly to blame, he felt others should do the same. So whilst he sympathised with callers regarding the 'invasion' as some put it, of the Travellers, and whilst he pledged that he would do all he could to get them off town property as soon as possible, he put the blame for their occupation of the Town Fields exactly where it lay. As most callers said they would be phoning the Mayor the instant they had ceased speaking to him, and as, no doubt, other councillors throughout the town were taking similar calls and diverting them in likewise fashion, then it was not difficult to assume that Myra Morrison was experiencing a quite dreadful evening.

"Serves her right, the stupid woman," Alec Conway muttered angrily to himself as that very same thought occurred to him.

The phone rang again in the hallway. The councillor, almost numb from the virtually unceasing assault from Alexander Graham Bell's infernal creation, glanced at his watch; five past ten – "Do they never let up?" he groaned to himself.

He lifted a receiver which felt about half a ton in weight. "Alec Conway," he muttered.

"Alec – this is Eve." His spirits suddenly shot skywards – the cycle of incessant complaining and moaning had been broken. It was Jill's sister Eve, who dwelt on the other side of Brendon Combe, and who, no doubt, wished to have a chat with his wife, at great length, as they did at least a couple of times a week.

"Hello, Eve – nice to hear from you. Everything well, I trust." He gave her no chance to reply before saying, "I'll fetch Jill; she's in the lounge watching television."

Eve's reply, however, was brisk, to the point and assailed him before he could leave the phone and hail his spouse. "No, don't get Jill, Alec. It's you I want to speak to. Do you know there are New Age Travellers camping out in the Town Fields. I've just been past there; I would estimate there are at least a dozen caravans and other vehicles parked in there – and scores of people walking about."

Alec Conway groaned out loud. Was it not time to resign from the council – with immediate effect?

Alan Foreman, the *Brendon Combe Echo*'s long serving Deputy Editor, and council reporter, who had spent more time at meetings than all but the longest serving members of the council, made a prediction – born of years of experience of somewhat similar situations – at the beginning of the meeting of the Properties Committee, which was to prove very accurate.

Seeing the issue of the cuckoo-like New Age Travellers in the Town Fields – hastily added to the agenda – as being one of the few items of any real interest to the readers of the *Echo*, he opined that the committee would talk about it, over it and beneath it for hours, and do nothing. Not that his view was necessarily a harsh criticism of the committee; it was simply that many years of sitting at the press desk at the back of the council chambers in the town itself, in draughty halls following the meandering deliberations of parish councils in the villages near Brendon Combe, and in the more ornate comfortable offices and chamber of the district council which were situated on top of a hill at the edge of the town, had taught him that when confronted with major issues, a policy of inaction was invariably that which most councillors talked themselves into – often at great length. Cynical though he had become, however, Foreman tended to alleviate the elected members of much of the blame; "It's not so much the people that are at fault, as the system," he would usually say. "There is much to be said in favour of grass root democracy, but it's the worst of all governmental systems for actually getting decisions made, and things done."

That the reporter was slightly inaccurate in one of his predictions – that the committee would discuss it for hours – was something of a surprise, though it was mainly due to the, as always, excellent chairmanship of Susan Matthews, who had the rare ability of seemingly giving everybody a chance to express their views, but never allowed a discussion to ramble on. Indeed, the meeting of the Properties Committee this particular evening turned out to be briefer than normal.

This was mainly due to the order of business. For whilst the item regarding the Travellers was clearly the dominant issue of the evening, it had, because of its lateness in occurring, been tacked on near the end of the agenda, just before 'any other business'. Thus on this occasion, the members hastened through the preceding ten agenda items desperate to get to the enticing 'juicy' one at the end. So issues such as the colour of the new curtains for the Town Hall windows and stage; the complaint from a tenant of one of the council owned shops that his store room was riddled with dry rot; the report of the working party who were looking at the need for a new filtration plant for the swimming pool; the question of a sex shop being permitted to take over the tenancy of another of the town council owned shops (decision deferred, without discussion, until the next meeting of the committee for more 'information', much to Alan Foreman's chagrin, as he had anticipated a good story coming out of this item for this week's edition of the paper), and other business, took a bare twenty minutes to get through, when normally it would have used up the best part of two hours.

So item twelve – "To note the presence of New Age Travellers in the Town Fields and to decide a course of action" – was rapidly upon them, and the committee members, all present except for the Mayor, almost en masse glanced to see that Alan Foreman had his pen poised, then addressed themselves to the vexatious, troublesome, delicious problem which confronted them.

Susan Matthews, knowing she would have to keep a tight rein on proceedings if the debate was not to degenerate into a verbal brawl, called for some legal guidance from the town clerk before she allowed discussion.

"Well, Madam Chairman," said Harold Newman, loudly clearing his throat, always his habit when he felt he had his back to the wall. "The problem is, there would seem there is little we can do – in law, that is. I've had a word with our solicitors about it and they say we are in a difficult position."

"They've been saying that about every problem we've brought to them over the past thirty years and more," opined Claude Partridge. "All part of their plan, that is to make everything appear difficult, take twice as long as is needed to do anything, four times as long to actually sort a problem out, then charge ten times as much as is reasonable. Rogues they are – as are all lawyers. If I had my way, Madam Chairman . . ."

"There's much truth in what Mr Partridge says, Madam

Chairman, but in this instance things are certainly somewhat complicated," gabbled Alec Conway, diving into the debate with rare haste. He was usually happy to let a debate warm up somewhat before he got involved in it, but in this instance he felt that Claude Partridge's long held, and deeply felt grudge, against the legal profession would get them nowhere. "The fact is, as I mentioned to you a little earlier, Madam Chairman, I took a touch of legal advice myself this morning through – well, certain sources open to me, in a totally informal way, and was advised that the removal, by legal means, of the Travellers from the Town Fields is going to be exceedingly difficult. We can only . . ."

"Exactly, Madam Chairman," interjected the town clerk. "Mr Conway makes the very same point that our solicitors made to me over the phone today. They did say, however, that they were not experts in the matter, and would, on our behalf, take advice from specialists in the field of . . . of . . . of this type of thing."

"What do you mean, they're not experts?" rasped Ian Morton, the Chairman of the Finance and General Purposes Committee, who sat in on the Property Committee meetings by virtue of his office. "They're solicitors, aren't they? And this is a matter law, is it not? It seems to me there's a great deal in what Mr Partridge says about the way they charge, but now it appears they charge a fortune for their services and still don't know the solution to the problems we bring them."

"Oh, that's a little unfair, Madam Chairman," cried Harold Newman, anxious to defend the reputation of Maynard, Oliver and Miller, the 'Miller' of whom was his brother-in-law. "Normally our solicitors are most efficient and quite prompt in all that they do. In this instance the circumstances are somewhat different – indeed, exceptionally rare, so they feel that they need to consult experts in the field of trespass etcetera, before they advise us as to what our next steps should be."

"And we'll have to pay fat fees to these so-called experts, Madam Chairman – right?" Claude Partridge, the most genial and courteous of men normally, once again gave vent, and became belligerent over the subject of council solicitors in particular, and all form of professional advisers in general.

"Well, naturally, Madam Chairman," snorted the town clerk, seeing nothing remotely wrong with such a thing.

"I'm afraid, on this occasion, I feel we have little option but to go along the avenue of our solicitors seeking expert advice," ruled Susan Matthews, anxious to put the matter into perspective before Claude Partridge fired a further broadside. "It is only fair to say we face a very considerable problem in removing these Travellers from the Town Fields, assuming, that is, they are not prepared to move on voluntarily. Perhaps they might well do so in a few days – let us hope so, at least. But it is only prudent to assume the worst – that they will not move, and that we have to find legal ways of making them. And the major problem in that direction is, as the town clerk and Mr Conway will no doubt confirm, both having had words with legal people today, that the Travellers were given permission to camp in the Fields by the Mayor of this town. Thus, at the moment, there's not a judge in the land who will grant any injunction to move them on, and the police, of course, will not – indeed, cannot – do anything without such authority from the courts."

"The police in this town don't do anything much even if they do have authority from the courts," grunted Claude Partridge, who, despite his aura of being an elderly, respectable semi-retired farmer, and something of a pillar of the local community, had a broad, uncompromising anti-authoritarian streak within him.

"No, what you say is entirely correct, Madam Chairman," agreed Alec Conway. "The brutal truth is that the Travellers are camped there quite legitimately – at present. The thing we've got to find out is when they lose legitimacy, and decide what we do when that day arrives."

"That's if they do ever lose legitimacy," contributed Hilary Spencer, a touch shyly. With her mere two months' experience on the council, and her relative youth, she was very much aware of being the junior member of the authority – even though nobody overtly treated her as such – and was always somewhat nervous when she spoke. "What if having been given permission, it means they can legally remain there for as long as they want to?"

"A very fair point, Mrs Spencer," agreed the chairman. "But

one, I fancy, too worrying to consider. Certainly one I don't feel there's any purpose in talking about at present. If that situation confronts us in the future, of course, then we will have to try to find some solution to it. At present, we must work on the theory – perhaps I should say, hope – that the Travellers do not have the right to be in the Fields despite the Mayor foolishly allowing them to be there, and seek the legal way to move them on."

"Yes, I fancy that's the way to approach it, Madam Chairman," agreed her vice chairman, Gordon Holland. "But whatever happens – even if we are successful – our legal bill is going to be enormous over this; so I propose that all legal costs incurred by this council over this issue should be passed on to the Mayor, Mrs Morrison, for payment. She got us into this, so it's up to her to get us out – and if it costs us a great deal of money to do so, as it will, then she should pay it."

"I second that, Madam Chairman," agreed Claude Partridge, enthusiastically. "Mr Holland is absolutely right. It's her stupidity that's got us into this mess, so it's her money that should get us out of it."

"I really do not think this is a fair proposal," ruled Susan Matthews. "Whilst I am not without some sympathy for the feelings which have been expressed, I'm sure the town clerk will agree with me that there is no local government act which would hold an individual member of a council financially responsible in a situation such as this. Is that not correct, Mr Newman?"

"Completely correct, I would say, Madam Chairman," agreed Harold Newman, trying hard to look infinitely more knowledgeable than he was. "I would say, as you have, that basically, even if a councillor acts foolishly, the costs to the council resulting from that act still have to be met out of public funds. However, if members want a ruling, I can consult our solicitors in the morning and get their professional opinion."

"They won't know – they'll have to call in an expert," snorted Alec Conway.

"And there'll be another enormous legal bill," said June Sullivan, who, whilst in no way connected with Maynard, Oliver and Miller, was married to a solicitor who was a partner in another firm. Thus, she well knew the system.

"Yes, quite so," agreed the chairman. "I think we'll not pursue legal advice in that direction at the moment, members."

"That's fair enough," agreed the vice chairman, "but I would still like my proposal put to the meeting; it's been formally proposed and seconded," he added a touch belligerently. Gordon Holland was still somewhat upset at not getting the Deputy Mayorship for the year.

Susan Matthews looked annoyed – a rare event; for she was aware that such a proposition at that time was a total irrelevance, and in no way assisted in tackling the problem of the Travellers. Still, she knew that the quickest way forward would be to put the proposition to the meeting; after all, there was no way it would get a majority.

"Very well," she snapped. "I put the proposition to the council that all legal expenses be charged to the Mayor. All in . . ."

"Just a moment, Madam Chairman," interjected Harold Newman. "I do question the wisdom of putting such a proposal. I mean, I'm sure it is not legal. And we really should not vote on illegal proposals, should we? Perhaps, if the members really wished to vote on such a proposal, I should get a ruling from our solicitors. That would be the safest way."

"Mr Newman, I've not the slightest intention of waiting a month till the next meeting of the Properties Committee to get a ruling from our solicitors on this matter," rasped the chairman, getting increasingly annoyed over the entire business. "I want to get the matter out of the way; if the proposition is illegal, then I will be the one they haul off to jail – all right." She fixed the town clerk with an angry glare, well aware that his main concern was that somewhere along the line, he might be held responsible for something or other which the council had done.

"Very well, Madam Chairman," he replied meekly, obviously relieved that if the roof fell in on Susan Matthews, not so much as a single tile would drop on his head.

"Right, I put the proposal to the committee. All those in favour – two. All those against – six. The motion is lost. Right, if we can move on, I would like to ask Mr Butler the present situation regarding the Travellers in the Town Fields – he has been monitoring things. How many are there, Mr Butler?"

The works manager, his mind indulging itself in a reverie regarding the holiday he was due to begin that following weekend, when he was off to Italy with his wife, reluctantly returned his attention to the meeting and to the ulcer inducing problem of the Travellers in the Town Fields.

"Well, Madam Chairman, I'm afraid their numbers appear to keep growing. There were eighteen vehicles there this morning, but I looked in there on the way to the meeting this evening and now there are twenty-three there. It's difficult to give an exact number of people, but I should say between forty to fifty – men, women and children."

"And are they making much mess?" enquired the chairman.

The works manager shrugged his shoulders. "Well, I suppose it could be worse," he said vaguely. "They'll cut up the football pitch a bit with their lorries, caravans, call them what you will. The ground's a bit soft there with all the rain we've had recently. Also, there's a bit of litter lying around – but not too much at present."

"I should hope not," snorted Gordon Holland, "they've only been there for about twenty-four hours. What's it going to be like after they've been there twenty-four days, that's what I'd like to know?"

An expression of horror flitted across the work manager's face, which was rapidly chased away by the thought of a fortnight's holiday beginning at the weekend; a look of consternation, if not horror, returned quickly when he realised that if the Travellers were indeed still around in twenty-four days' time, he would also be around once more, his vacation a rapidly receding memory. "I shudder to think, Madam Chairman," he replied, shaking his head sadly at the nightmarish prospect.

"As do we all, Mr Butler," retorted the chairman. "Still, it is to be hoped that long before then this problem will have ceased to exist. As it is, I don't think there is much more we can do this evening."

"Much more we an do?" snorted Gordon Holland. "But we've

done nothing at all, Madam Chairman."

"Not directly, no, Mr Holland. But we have had an exchange of views here, and I think we all realise that at present our position as a council is, shall we say – difficult. Whilst I am as reluctant as the members of this committee to spend money we can ill afford on expert legal advice, I feel that this is possibly the only way forward at present. Frankly, I fancy we are in the business of looking for legal loopholes at the moment, and only those qualified in such matters can point them out to us. Hopefully, by the time the full council meets in a fortnight's time, we shall be in possession of legal weapons with which to legitimately move these Travellers off council property."

"I shudder to think what state the Town Fields will be in in a fortnight's time if these wretched Travellers are still there," groaned June Sullivan.

"Oh, they'll still be there all right," muttered Claude Partridge. "And in their droves I don't wonder."

"And the vandalism they'll perpetrate," rasped Ian Morton, "and the cost of putting it right."

"And the disease they could spread," cried Gordon Holland. "God alone knows what sort of epidemics folk like that can spread – I mean they never work; and the way they live; Why, I've heard that . . ."

"I really do not feel that this is relevant, ladies and gentlemen," interjected the chairman hastily, seeing Alan Foreman scribbling away at the back of the chamber at a frenetic pace. There had already been alarmist talk to fill almost half the *Echo* and put local folk in fear of their safety; if she allowed such a ludicrous discussion to continue, there would soon be mass panic in the streets. "I propose to move on to the next item on the agenda – 'any other business'."

She glanced sideways at the clerk. "I've not been notified of anything, Mr Newman."

"There's nothing as far as I am aware, Madam Chairman. However, I would . . ."

"Good," snapped Susan Matthews. "I therefore declare the meeting closed and thank you all for your attendance."

Harold Newman, in the process of telling the chairman that he needed to fix a date for a meeting of the working party set up to draw up a list of new grass and maintenance equipment needed for the Town Fields, had been cut short. He shrugged his shoulders and dropped his pen to the desk in front of him. Well, they could fix a date at full council. Perhaps it would be best to leave it for the time being anyway, he mused as he began to sort out the detritus of paperwork before him; after all, the least said about the Town Fields – in any context – the best at present.

Alec Conway said his 'goodnights', and was just passing through the chamber doorway, when he was hailed by Colin Butler.

"Alec – about that seat."

"Oh yes – any joy?"

"Not really. I contacted Sam Simpson in the maintenance department up the district council and, initially, he said he would get one of their contractors to repair it. I couldn't believe my luck, to be honest. I mean, things are rarely that simple when it comes to dealing with the district."

"And I fancy you're going to tell me this was no exception in the long run."

"I'm afraid you're right. Today Sam phoned me to say they would not be able to fix the seat after all as they didn't own it. He reckons they've never owned any seats in Brendon Combe – which is nonsense, of course. I'm certain they own those two – and I told him so. I mean it stands to reason that they'll own the one on the far side of the wall, I was speaking about – not the broken one that is, the other. Because when I was giving that a check over a few days after you complained to me concerning the dangerous one, I noticed it was placed there in memory of Albert Peacock who was chairman of the district council for some years immediately following the War. So it stands to reason that as he was being remembered for services rendered to the district council, then it's their responsibility to maintain it."

"Possibly, Colin," replied Alec, cautiously, "but you and I know full well that logic and the workings of local government – like logic and the law," he added, his magisterial experiences briefly flitting across his mind, "do not always go hand in hand."

"Fair comment," agreed the works manager, "but in this instance I'm sure they own those two seats and are just trying to get out of doing anything about them. 'Cause, you see, Alec, Sam Simpson put his foot in it without realising it. He said to me – as I told you just now – that the district had never owned those seats, then he went on to say that a letter had been sent to the town council from the legal department at the district, that the town council was responsible for the maintenance of all seats, no matter which authority put them there in the first place. So if they never owned them to start with, what need was there for such a letter. No, they own them all right – they're just trying to evade responsibility, and save a few quid."

"And have we received a letter?"

"God knows – Harold Newman certainly doesn't," snorted Butler. "He says he can't recall ever receiving such a letter, but you know Harold– he doesn't know the day of the week half the time. How he's managed to hold onto his job all these years I really . . ." The works manager's voice tailed off, he suddenly realising that he was, perhaps, saying a little more than he should.

Alec Conway ignored Butler's obvious contempt for the town clerk; such was well known anyway. And it was a problem which would disappear within the next two years when Newman was due to retire – thus a new clerk would be appointed. And the probability was that it would be a man or woman closer to Butler's age and outlook, the very real difference in those vital twin elements – the present town clerk being almost twenty years older than Butler – being the major obstacles to their achieving any true rapport during the time they had served together; they were men of different generations, different values, different priorities, and both stubborn. Both had served the town valiantly, and to the best of their ability – Butler, in his field, probably superior to Newman in his – but they had always performed as individuals, rather than as a team.

"So the reality is, Colin, that we still do not know, officially, who owns that blasted seat," snapped Conway, anxious to move the conversation to a conclusion, then get home.

"Well, I would say that we certainly know who owns it, but we can not get anybody to take responsibility for it," replied the works manager with a mighty sigh.

"And you're certain it doesn't belong to the town council?"

"Positive. I've checked through all my records – took a fair old time to find them all to tell you the truth, but Gloria in the office has been very helpful as always. Anyway, according to the records – and they go back thirty years, so well before my time – – we own all the seats in the town, except for these two, and the district council own those."

"And they say they don't."

"Precisely. But I'm not going to let them get away with it, Alec. They've either got to repair that seat or replace it, or even, perhaps give us the money to put it right – don't you think?" added he, seeking reassurance.

"Damned right, Colin. If it's theirs, they've got to sort it out. But don't let it all go on for too long, will you? Old Arthur Burdon'll have my guts drying in the noonday sun if something isn't done soon – and, even worse, his vote will be lost to me for ever."

"Don't worry, Alec. Leave it with me; I'll get it sorted out."

So, although a touch apprehensive as to the works manager's ability to bring, swiftly, fresh wood to the seat – efficient fellow though he generally was – the councillor went for his only real option by doing the man's bidding, and leaving it to him.

The July meeting of the Brendon Combe Town Council produced a press desk well overflowing with six journalists in all – three from papers covering the town, district or county, and a further trio from national newspapers. Indeed, longer serving members of the authority could only remember one occasion when a meeting attracted more from the press, and that was twelve years previously when a leading lady councillor had been caught in a caravan on a site a couple of miles out of town with a District Council Planning Officer. The 'big fish' from Fleet Street had, on that occasion, had their time wasted, as the female councillor in question had submitted her apologies for the evening, claiming she was suffering from flu, whilst the subject of her behaviour with the planning officer had not been raised as it was judged by the then Mayor – quite rightly – that as the councillor and officer belonged to different authorities, their behaviour was in no way the business of the town council (although disapproval had been forthcoming from several members of the council who had felt that the councillor's behaviour had brought embarrassment to the authority). The lady in question remained a member of the council for the two years or so which remained before the next elections. But then, good councillor though she was, she had fallen foul of an electorate with longish memories, and had not been re-elected. As to the planning officer, he had sought, successfully, a position on another and larger, council, with which he was still employed, and had reached a very senior position.

And likewise this turned out to be another barren evening for the ladies and gentlemen of the press, who were sensing sensational happenings from a council with a 'Hippie' Mayor at the helm (as one tabloid had already described Myra Morrison) and a public park 'teeming with debauched New Age Travellers', as another had put it. For with the Gods once more being exceedingly kind to the Mayor, she was legitimately not present at the meeting, a conference and seminar for all Mayors or Chairmen of Councils in Devon being held at County Hall, Exeter, that very day, continuing – according to the agenda – until 9pm.

There were murmurings amongst members of the council that the issues confronting the authority at that time, were vastly more important than indulging in the banal twaddle which would probably be dominating the deliberations taking place at County Hall – "A waste of time and ratepayers' money," as Claude Partridge put it, being far too long in the tooth to use the modern terminology of 'council tax payers'. Myra Morrison though, could claim, with total legitimacy, that she had a duty to the council and the local community to see they were fully represented at such an important gathering. Also, she could further argue that there was a perfectly able Deputy Mayor available to conduct meetings in her absence; that, after all, was amongst the functions a Deputy Mayor was there to fulfil. And

135

Gerald Dunlop occupied the chair with an authoritative ease surprising in a man who had been on the council but a couple of years, and had never even held a vice-chairmanship of any committee. Having said that, he had been chairman of the amateur operatic society for a few years, giving that up only when he went onto the council – or so he explained to Alec Conway when the long serving councillor had congratulated him at the end of the council meeting on the way he had handled things.

"After that experience, Alec," he said, grinning broadly, "anything else is simple."

Still, in reality, the meeting was not a particularly difficult one to chair, for very little happened or was discussed. Harold Newman, with Colin Butler still away on holiday, reported that there were now thirty-one vehicles parked in the Town Fields which were 'being inhabited', as he quaintly put it. As to numbers, there were 'several' Travellers of 'all ages' there now – a description which brought a thunderous response from Councillor Peter Renton – a man who liked facts and, not unreasonably, expected accuracy from officials.

"What for heaven's sake is 'several' Deputy Mayor?" he rasped. "Twenty, fifty, a hundred? To use such a ludicrously vague word is of no help at all."

"Well, I cannot give an exact number, Mr Deputy Mayor," retorted the town clerk in clipped, somewhat hurt tones. "I mean I did not have a head count – to have done so would have been extremely difficult and very time consuming. It took me some time to ascertain the number of actual vehicles – they are not parked in an orderly fashion, Mr Deputy Mayor, as I'm sure Mr Renton is aware. I do not feel that it would be a responsible use of public money for me to use my time in trying to count the exact number of people there, especially when they keep moving about."

"I reckon old Harold was scared of them," scoffed Michael Davey – who was an ex-wrestler and built like a granite wall – to Alec Conway sitting beside him. It was unlikely that Councillor Davey had ever been scared of anyone during his entire life – and if all else failed, he would be the council member best equipped

136

to handle, organise and carry out the more unorthodox method which could be needed to evict the Travellers from the Town Fields.

"I've got some sympathy with him, to be fair," conceded Conway. "There are some right looking hard cases amongst those Travellers – as far as I can see, anyway."

"It's rarely the tough looking ones you need to worry about, Alec," muttered the big fellow, probably accurately.

Conway nodded his acceptance of the point just as the town clerk, his face registering a mixture of emotions from agony to bereavement as he tried to estimate the number of Travellers in the Town Fields, came up with a classic statement as to the amount.

"Well, I reckon there are at least seventy of them there – although then again there could be more. Mind you, I suppose there might not be quite as many."

Peter Renton groaned out loud, but was unable to deliver a broadside of the articulate, acerbic, blood draining invective for which he was noted on the council, due to a hasty intervention by the Deputy Mayor. "Well, I suppose that gives us some idea, Mr Newman. Obviously there are a considerable number of Travellers in the Town Fields, and their ranks appear to be ever swelling."

"Of course they do, Mr Deputy Mayor." The soft but firm tones were those of Malcolm Turner, an excellent councillor held in high esteem by most other members, Alec Conway included. "And their numbers will continue to grow unless we take firm action to evict them." The only problem with the man was that he was unfortunate enough to be married to a woman who was, possibly, Brendon Combe's biggest snob, and whom had angered Jill Conway to such an extent a few years earlier that Alec took care at all social events involving the council, to steer clear of Malcolm Turner if they both were accompanied by their spouses – which was a pity, as the dentist was good, amusing company, despite the slight arrogance which often characterised his demeanour.

"Now I thought, in my simple innocence, Mr Deputy Mayor," continued Turner, "that the town clerk was going to report to us tonight as to the progress our solicitors in consultation with the so-called experts in this particular field of law, had made towards finding rulings or a loophole in this law through which we will be able to shuffle the Travellers off the hallowed turf that is the Town Fields. So far all we've had is a formal report and a most vague intimation as to how many Travellers are actually in the Fields, but no mention as to the amount of mess they are creating and damage they are doing down there – although our own eyes, even from a distance, tell us that it is considerable – and not so much as a word concerning the progress, or, I fear, lack of it in actually getting these wretched people removed."

Eyes which had been riveted upon Malcolm Turner as he spoke, immediately, following Malcolm resuming his seat, focused upon the town clerk – who was looking singularly unhappy.

"Well unfortunately, Mr Deputy Mayor, there is nothing really to report at the moment," he stuttered.

"How long is it all going to take, Mr Deputy Mayor?" rasped an angry Claude Partridge. "They've already been deliberating for over a fortnight."

"This is a very complex issue, Mr Deputy Mayor," Newman replied, attempting to avoid actually looking at any particular councillor, by keeping his eyes fixed firmly upon the blank wall at the back of the chamber as he did habitually when the problems vastly outnumbered the solutions. "That's something, I would have thought, of which members would be very much aware. As things stand, the expert legal firm which our solicitors are consulting have felt it prudent to seek the opinion of a – well – well – Queen's Counsel who is well versed in such matters. Hopefully he . . ."

"A Queen's Counsel?" Claude Partridge's voice was almost strangulated with a volatile mixture of incredulity and rage. "Did the town clerk say, a Queen's Counsel?"

"I fancy he did, Mr Partridge," replied Gordon Dunlop in as level a tone of voice as he could muster.

"But it'll cost us a fortune," ranted the veteran councillor. "Good God, these people will charge you a couple of hundred quid to tell you the time of day. It seems to me, Mr Deputy Mayor, that if we've got to go along the road of QCs and so on, then we might as well wipe our hands of the entire business and let these infernal Travellers stay there until they decide they want to go. No matter how much damage they cause, it'll probably not cost us as much as our legal fees if we've taken the advice of people such as this."

"Mr Deputy Mayor, if we want to get the New Age Travellers out of the Town Fields, then we have to be fully armed in terms of the law," retorted the town clerk. "For reasons which we are all too well aware, our case is not that strong, so we really do need to take advice from lawyers at the very highest level even though, naturally, such advice will prove to be expensive. If you want my opinion, Mr Deputy Mayor, I feel . . ."

"Thank you, Mr Newman," snapped Gerald Dunlop, cutting off the town clerk in full flow; he did not particularly want the town clerk's advice, nor did he want a sterile discussion on the Travellers to drag on for hours when, essentially – except for their numbers, and the level of mess and damage they were causing, increasing – nothing had changed during the two weeks since the meeting of the Properties Committee.

"I think we all know what the present situation is," continued the Deputy Mayor, "and I feel there is nothing to be gained by continuing this debate at the moment. However, I am sure I speak for all members of the council and, of course, the people of Brendon Combe, when I say that this entire business represents a deplorable situation, with our Town Fields virtually hi-jacked by these wretched people, and it is essential that our legal representatives report to us urgently and advise us as to how we are going to rid ourselves of these pests. And I mean urgently – we cannot go on like this. So what I would propose, members, is that as soon as the town clerk has clear advice from our lawyers as to the way forward – and that needs to be very, very soon," – he glared at a somewhat sheepish looking Newman, as he said the words – "we call an extraordinary meeting of the full council to discuss the matter further. Do members agree?"

Generally impressed by the way Dunlop had summed up the

situation, put the town clerk in his place and generally controlled the meeting, members did, indeed agree with the proposal, though with differing degrees of enthusiasm. Claude Partridge, in particular, was still convinced that the involvement of a Queen's Counsel would put the town council in the hands of the official receiver.

With the Traveller problem put on the 'back burner' for the time being, the national reporters quickly left the meeting, their notebooks scarcely scratched, to be followed almost immediately by the others, with the exception of Alan Foreman, whose dedication to duty had long since meant he was a credit to his profession. He was rewarded to some extent that whilst he gained nothing dramatic or spectacular for the upcoming edition of the *Echo*, he was able to fill a few column inches with the news that after taking months to decide the colour of the new town hall window and stage curtains, the entire issue had to be returned to the relevant working party for further consideration because they had taken so long to make a decision, the colour and the type of material chosen had ceased production. He was also able to report that one of the hanging baskets put up outside of the Town Hall to enhance the beauty of the town centre, had fallen on an elderly lady's head, and she was in the process of suing the council – and also that the Brownies were given permission to hold their annual sports day in the Town Fields, weather and New Age Travellers permitting.

One thing he would not be able to report on, though, was a forthcoming meeting of the Swimming Pool Working Party called urgently to discuss further deterioration in the condition of the pool which had been built, most controversially, at enormous expense by the town council some six years previously. Rumours abounded in the town that there were major problems with the filtration plant, the water heating system, and even worse, that the building itself, quite new though it was, had developed leaks in both ceiling and walls.

Working parties always met in camera, but Alan Foreman had been around local government sufficiently long to sniff a good story evolving from a series of meetings of the working party

140

during the past couple of months, and was quite prepared to wait for the story to come out – which it had to very soon, of that he was convinced. Council problems, plus money wasted, plus possible inefficiency, plus the inevitable public anger, meant a few front page stories and a letters' page crammed full for weeks to come as far as the genial, but ever cynical, deputy editor was concerned.

A hot, thundery Friday morning, some ten days after the meeting of the full council found Alec Conway walking through the town on his way to the magistrate's court. During the time which had elapsed since the meeting, there had been no word from the council's legal experts regarding a successful finding of the loophole which would see them able to evict the New Age Travellers from the Town Fields.

Throughout this period of council inaction, the number of Travellers had grown even further, with possibly as many as ninety camping there now. Strangely, however, as the numbers of the Travellers had grown, the amount of complaints about them seemed to have decreased. Certainly from Alec Conway's point of view, whereas during the early days of their coming to the Fields he had received a monsoon of phone calls, the amount now had reduced to a decidedly modest number – and he was no longer almost afraid to answer the phone. Possibly the main reason for this was that most people in the town were only too well aware that the Mayor was the one directly responsible for the coming of the New Age Travellers; thus, whilst she had tried to atone somewhat for her mid-summer madness by making a statement, the previous week, which was carried in the local papers and on local radio, that she felt it was time for the Travellers to move on, the fair minded majority of the townsfolk fully appreciated that there was little the council could do to get the Travellers out of the Town Fields – and the town.

Also the Travellers had caused relatively little trouble in the town. Their behaviour had been, generally, acceptable in terms of public order, and whilst they had made some mess in the Town Fields – and by their very presence discouraged local folk from using them in the customary way – this was due more to their ever increasing numbers than to any acts of vandalism or wanton slovenliness. Just as well, he mused to himself as he turned the corner and came in view of the church, for it could be that the people of Brendon Combe were destined to cohabit with the Travellers for a fair time yet to come.

"Alec – they've still not repaired this seat." His reverie was broken, painfully – and he knew by whom before he even looked. Arthur Burdon was standing beside the seat in the church wall on the opposite side of the street. Seeing that he had attracted the councillor's attention, he half turned towards the seat and pointed in its direction – with no small measure of drama. "The fact is, Alec," continued he in stentorian tones, "it's worse than the last time I spoke to you about it. In fact, it looks to me as if it could collapse at any moment."

It was a statement which did contain a measure of exaggeration, confirmed by the fact that old Mrs Bradstone, secretary of the Pensioners' Association, and rather a large lady, was seated in the middle of the bench, seemingly comfortably and in no apparent danger of plunging through its rotting timbers. However, the good lady, never backwards in coming forwards when it came to airing grievances – her own or anybody else's – did not allow her present apparently safe comfort to come between herself and her support of Arthur Burdon.

"Yes, Alec – this seat is in the most terrible state. To tell you the truth, I'm half terrified sitting on it. In fact, I fancy I can feel it slowly giving way underneath me. The trouble is, with my heart – and my veins – the doctor won't let me stand up for long. He's always telling me to sit down and relax a bit more – but how can a woman relax sitting on a seat that's falling to pieces? I'm worried sick it might collapse any second and do me a mischief. I really don't know how the council haven't done something about it. I thought you'd have done something about it by now," she admonished him. "I always vote for you, you know."

"Thanks, Mrs Bradstone – appreciated, that is. I'm sorry about the condition of this seat. A shocking state and no mistake – as I said to Arthur here when he pointed it out to me a few weeks back. But the good news is that it's all in hand. I've reported it to the works manager, Colin Butler, and he's in the process of sorting it out."

"How long does it take to sort out something which, I would have thought, should take virtually no time to put right," argued the somewhat aggressive Burdon. "It's weeks and weeks ago I pointed it out to you, and still nothing's been done. Dammit all, Alec, any decent carpenter could put this seat to rights in half a day, less, probably – that's if the existing wood will take a nail. If it won't, then all that's needed is for the remains of this one to be hauled off and a new one put in its place – which would take about half an hour."

"True – true, Arthur," agreed the councillor, hastily. "The one small problem at the moment, though, is that Colin Butler can't fully establish who owns the seat. Apparently it's not owned by the town council, but is almost certainly the property of the district. The trouble is, they say it's nothing to do with them – but then, councils always say things like that. It's a way of getting out of meeting their responsibilities. I've no doubt that we'll soon be able to convince them that it's their seat and that they've got to get it repaired. Shouldn't take long now; Colin Butler is a first class chap – he'll soon get it all sorted out." He glanced at Arthur Burdon, then at Mrs Bradstone, and witnessed expressions of doubt, bordering on disbelief. He couldn't blame them. It was, after all, none too convincing a tale – but it was the best his generally fertile mind could come up with. The truth was, he had not the slightest idea as to how soon the seat would receive attention, but he hoped, for the sake of his own peace – and the 'old folk' vote – it would not be too long. He glanced at his watch. "Dear me, look at the time," said he, somewhat lamely. "I'd better be off or I'll be late for court."

"Plead guilty but insane, Alec – they'll believe you," guffawed Arthur Burdon.

The magistrate returned a somewhat sickly smile. The joke had been funny the first time he had heard it – many light years before. "Yes, reckon you're about right there, Arthur," he agreed, taking the easy way out. "Anyway, I must go – and I'll keep chasing them about the seat," he promised as he moved off in the direction of the old court building some 200 yards up the street.

"And don't forget about the ladies' toilets," Mrs Bradstone shouted after him. He came to an abrupt halt and swung around.

"The ladies' toilets?" he enquired.

"Yes – the state they're in. Didn't I say? – No – I don't think I did. Well, Alec, its the 'Ladies' – just the other side of the Town Hall. I went in them yesterday, and they were in the most deplorable state imaginable. They did not look as if they had been cleaned for weeks; there was toilet paper all over the place – and the disgusting things somebody had written on the walls; well, words fail me." Not for long, however, because before the councillor could give a reply, she was off again. "Something's got to be done about them, Alec. They need a real clean up in every way, and then they need to be kept to a decent standard. I mean, there are quite a few tourists who come to this town – because we're close to Dartmoor, and suchlike; what will they think when they see the state of them?"

"Bugger the tourists," responded Arthur Burdon with some belligerence. "It's us, the local council tax payers that pay for their maintenance, not the tourists – so it's us that have the right to expect them to be clean and tidy. Speaking of tourists, I reckon it's them that makes the toilets filthy to start with – and vandalise them. The Gents are just the same."

"Fair enough," retorted Conway; "leave it with me. I'll get on to the environmental health department up at the district council the minute I get out of court – speaking of which, I must dash or I'll be shot. Take care." He turned on his heels and began to half run up the street, his worries concerning being late being all too real.

"Bye, Alec," called out Mrs Bradstone in a quite cheery voice directed at his receding figure. "I can leave the toilets to you then, can I?"

He half turned, raised a hand in acknowledgement, said, "Yes leave it with me, Mrs Bradstone, I'll sort it out," then continued on towards the court, writing as he scurried along, a brief note in a small diary he always carried with him, to do something about the toilets; the Secretary of the Pensioners' Association was not the sort of person to let down if a man was anxious to retain the crucial support, electorally, of the elderly community of the town.

Conway reached the stone stairway which curved up to the magistrates' retiring room, and hastened up. It was almost five minutes to ten, and he always liked to be there by a quarter to ten at the latest so that he, along with the other magistrates, would get a reasonably leisurely briefing as to what the morning held in store.

Generally he enjoyed his work on the bench, although when originally he had been asked to allow his name to be put forward for it all those years before, he had taken quite a long time to agree. Not that it was particularly onerous in terms of time, generally half a day, once a fortnight – usually a Friday. But he had been a little uneasy as to whether or not he had the qualities necessary to sit in judgement of others. Maud Campbell, however, the mother of an old school friend of his – long since gone from Devon to make his fortune (which he had largely achieved, apparently) – who was retiring from the bench because she had reached seventy, the compulsory retiring age, had persuaded him that he would be an ideal candidate to become a Justice of the Peace. "You're the right age, Alec," she had said. "They're looking for people in their thirties these days. Also, you're a man, and we badly need another man as there are more women than men on the bench at present. And, of course, you're a local man who knows our ways, and the people in the area – another major plus. You are hard working, as well, you're clearly no fool and, to my knowledge, you've never been in any trouble with the law." So that was it; according to Mrs Campbell, these were the necessary requirements for the post, and the fact that many other men in the town would have fulfilled such conditions meant nothing as far as she was concerned. She knew Alec Conway, felt he would make a good magistrate, so duly encouraged him to fill in his application forms, and along with a close friend of hers on the bench – who scarcely knew him at all – signed the forms as referees.

Then, to his eternal surprise, he received, some six months later, a letter from the Lord Chancellor's department in London, telling him that he had been appointed as a JP to sit on Brendon Combe Bench – to judge his peers and to sign passport applications, gun licence forms and myriad other official documents. Indeed, he often felt that the form signing part of it, which he would do for nothing whereas a solicitor would invariably charge a fee, was the most constructive and helpful contribution he made to local society, the actual administration of justice increasingly becoming a red tape laden, paper burdened, costly, inefficient, uncaring lottery.

He reached the top of the scruffy, paint chipped, dingy stairwell and opened the heavy oak door facing him. "Morning all," said he cheerfully, as he entered the retiring room. "Sorry I'm late – had my ear bent over council matters, as usual."

"New Age Travellers, Alec, I would imagine," opined Alison Bentham, a pleasant woman in her early sixties, who would be chairing the court.

"No – ladies' toilets and broken seats, actually; and gents' toilets, as well," he replied. "Mercifully, it's gone quite quiet on the Traveller front at present – thank heavens. Not that I expect it to last – as long as they remain in the Town Fields, it is going to be a recurring problem – perhaps even nightmare."

"Well, sadly Alec, that nightmare is about to envelop you," said John Killick – the third magistrate sitting that day – with a grin. "The court's crawling with them this morning."

"What – we've got them in court!" Conway was stunned by such news. "Why's that, for heaven's sake? I mean, there's not so such as a mention about them on the court list." Was there no escape from these wretched people? – was the thought which fleetingly dominated the councillor's mind.

"No, you are quite correct, sir – they're not on the court list." The words were spoken by Andrew Parsons, Clerk and Legal Adviser to the Court, a quiet, genial and highly efficient man of some forty years of age. A staunch believer in the traditional formalities, he would always address members of the bench with a deferential 'sir' or 'ma'am' in the environs of the court, whilst – in Alec Conway's case, at least – addressing them by their first names outside of it. "The fact is, the police had a blitz on them down in the Town Fields yesterday morning, and they've all been hauled in today – before they move on, I suppose."

"Chance would be a fine thing," snorted Conway.

"Yes – too nice a spot, the Town Fields, for them to give it up that easily, I would have thought," agreed John Killick, in the level, considered way which made him such a good magistrate.

"What have they been up to, Mr Parsons," enquired Alison Bentham, getting to the heart of the matter as was her custom.

"Nothing dramatic, Ma'am," replied he, calmly. "My experience of any of these travelling folk – gypsies, tinkers, even New Age Travellers – is that they're rarely involved in any real crime, except a bit of petty pilfering; or, at least, are rarely caught indulging in it. No, it's usually motoring offences with them – and these New Age people are terrors for it. No driving licences, no MOTs, no road tax and of course, the really important one, no insurance – that's their lay of the land, of that you can be sure. So our local constabulary must have known they'd be in for rich pickings when they had their raid yesterday; it'll certainly have done wonders for their crime statistics."

"Yes, it'll have done that, all right," agreed Killick. "It must be like manna from heaven for them in that sense."

"And it will be a great boost to their success rate as well, sir," the clerk observed. "Not the hardest thing in the world to prove, is it, whether or not you are MOT'd, taxed, insured or have a driving licence. You can either produce the documentation, or you cannot. And if you cannot, then you're in trouble, with a conviction virtually assured. Anyway, no fewer than thirty-eight New Age Travellers were unable to produce documents of various importance; indeed, some were unable to produce any documents at all. So they've all been summoned to appear in court today. And looking at the public benches five minutes ago, it would appear that most of them have actually come – and brought their families with them, many of them at any rate. A colourful sight in many instances, that I must say." A man most tolerant of human nature and the possessor of a sound sense of perspective, was Andrew Parsons.

"I'm surprised so many have turned up," said the chairman.

"Well, I suppose it makes a bit of a change for them, ma'am," replied the clerk. "Not that a goodly number of them are strangers to the inside of courtrooms, I don't suppose. I mean, if they've got no documents now, then they've probably had none for years – perhaps never. In a lot of places, of course, they get away with it, because the police are only interested in moving them on – and clearly you cannot move somebody on whilst also insisting that they appear in court, locally, a few days afterwards."

"Perhaps our local constabulary thought that the bundle of summonses they issued yesterday would have had the effect of getting them to move on immediately – rather than appear in court today," mused John Killick.

"As I said just now, though, a mere appearance in court is not going to be sufficient to make them vacate a high quality, all amenity laid-on site such as the Town Fields, especially when – which, I understand, is the crux of the matter – they can claim, technically, to be there legitimately, having been invited to occupy it by the Mayor of the town. Would you not agree, Alec?"

"I would, John – entirely," nodded the councillor. "I fancy that if they were camped down there totally illegally, then the crop of summonses might well have been sufficient to make them pack their bags and leave overnight. But they're well aware that no matter what happens today, it in no way affects the fact that they have been given the right to camp in the Town Fields."

"That is absolutely true, sir," agreed the clerk. "There is, however, another aspect to this affair – as I see it: The great majority of these people here today – perhaps all of them – will plead guilty. There's not much else they can do. As I said just now, either you've got your insurance, MOT, tax and so on, or you haven't. Now, if guilty, then the bench has few options in terms of sentencing. Obviously, you give them penalty points, whether they have a licence or not, and, generally – certainly it has always been the policy of this bench – a monetary penalty: And the fact that they are Travellers doesn't mean they have no money. The opposite, probably, for most of them will be making a few pounds out of scrap, buying and selling old cars and suchlike, plus it's a virtual certainty that the great majority will be claiming benefits from the state. In fact, with no rent or rates, or suchlike, to pay – certainly no mortgage – most of them probably will be better off than a goodly percentage of the local people who come before you for motoring offences or no TV licences and so forth. Therefore it is quite logical for you to impose reasonably substantial fines upon them – quite logically and totally fair; or course, that is, obviously, a matter for your worships to decide. They, for their part, naturally have the right to ask for time in which to pay. It would not be reasonable – in principle at any rate – to ask them to pay three figure amounts there and then. So, if given seven, fourteen, perhaps even twenty-eight days in which to pay, it would be in their interest to move on well before the end of the time they had been given, for they know, as do we all, that once they have moved out of the immediate area where the fine was imposed, the police of that district will have neither the time, nor inclination, to go in hot pursuit to obtain the fines they owe the court."

"So, the town would be rid of the New Age Travellers at last," mused John Killick.

"Legally, sir, they would have moved away with the intention, probably, of avoiding paying their fines," opined the clerk, judiciously. "However, which would be more advantageous to the local community – the Travellers remaining in a council park, but paying their dues to the court, all of which, of course, goes to the Government's coffers at Whitehall, or they moving on and releasing a widely used portion of very pleasant parkland at a time of year which it is most in demand, with the children being on their school summer holidays? That, of course, is a matter of personal opinion. From the legal point of view, naturally the court would expect them to either stay and pay their fines – or to move on and do so. Our receipt of their money is the sole matter that would interest us – not from where they sent it." Andrew Parsons smiled in his gentle, though shrewd way, then sat back in his chair.

There was silence for a few seconds as the three magistrates absorbed the implications of what the court clerk was saying. It was broken by Alec Conway. "It seems to me, you know, that it might well be somewhat improper for me to sit on the cases involving the New Age Travellers, being as I am a member of the town council."

Andrew Parsons nodded his agreement. "There is something in what you say, sir – if I may make so bold as to put forward an opinion," he added, deferentially. "Technically, or course, there would be no obligation on your part to step down from the bench on this issue today. The town council is not involved directly – indeed, not really involved at all. The offences are all against the Road Traffic Acts, and would be brought by the police no matter where the Travellers were camped at present. Having said that, though, I feel it my duty, as the bench's legal adviser, to say that with all the widespread publicity this business has had involving the town council, and Mayor and so forth – even in the national press, I'm led to believe – it would probably be better for the image of justice, if not its implementation, for you not to sit this morning. It is, though, entirely a matter for yourself, and, of course, for Mrs Bentham and Mr Killick."

"It is a matter for us, certainly," agreed the chairman, "but, for myself, I feel your advice is correct, Mr Parsons – and your feelings about not sitting in tune with my own, Alec. What do you think John?"

"Oh, I feel it would be most improper and, frankly, counter productive from everyone's point of view, for you to sit, Alec, for no matter what we decided, people would say that you were wearing your 'council hat' and that the course of justice was bent – if not perverted – to suit the council's ends. It would not be true, of course, but that wouldn't matter – the perception is what would matter. No, have a morning off, Alec – that would be best all round."

Alec Conway smiled, then nodded his head. "Fair enough," said he, briskly. "It certainly makes sense. I'll wend my way, then – unless there's anything I can lend a hand with. There are quite a large number of cases on the list."

"Nothing of any note, sir," replied the clerk. "A great deal of it – the bulk, in fact – is being adjourned, as per usual these days, and . . ."

"Not again," groaned Alison Bentham. "Does anything these days actually get to be heard?" The words were more a statement of frustration than a question needing an answer.

"Well, they do in the end, ma'am," opined Andrew Parsons, "but it does take a ludicrous amount of time nowadays. To be fair, both sides are to blame for these delays; for whilst it used to be the defence, almost invariably, which slowed matters down with constant requests for adjournments, for, often, the most trifling of reasons, we find in the office now that the prosecution is not greatly better. Still, ours not to reason why, as the saying goes."

"So really there's nothing that Alec can help us with," stated Alison Bentham, aware that the clock showed five minutes past ten – the hour when the court was due to start.

"Nothing, ma'am," confirmed the clerk. "Certainly there is nothing on the list which cannot be handled by two magistrates – most of which you'll actually deal with this morning, besides the Traveller's cases, are postal pleas of guilty in motoring cases, and likewise regarding TV licences. Oh, and there'll be half a dozen means inquiries, mostly for unpaid fines – although I believe there's one fellow in for maintenance arrears. So that's it; there are definitely no 'not guilties' which would require a third magistrate, of course – so two can handle everything with no problem."

The chairman smiled in the direction of the councillor. "That's it then, Alec – you're let off."

"I won't argue, Alison," said he, smiling broadly in return. "I can think of many better things to be doing this morning than sitting trying to mete out justice to hairy Travellers.

"And that's just the women," laughed John Killick, indulging in a brief flash of humour which, on the rare occasions he displayed it – and at its best – could be quick, incisive but never unkind. Alec Conway snorted in amusement, opened the door leading to the stairs, raised his hand in farewell, wished the remaining trio a 'pleasant morning', and was soon down the stairs and out into the warm mid-summer sunshine.

*　　*　　*　　*

Alec Conway was feeling in good spirits as he sat on the patio of his neat house on a pleasant though somewhat cool, early August evening, gazing out over his colourful, well kept garden. This seemingly ever changing, yet ever fresh splash of colour was due entirely to Jill who was brilliantly 'green fingered' and always managed to maintain a wide range of pigments to both the front and back gardens of the three bedroomed house, from the coming of the crocuses in late February to the final fading of the chrysanthemums in early November.

Certainly the councillor could never recall seeing the garden look better. This was due, possibly, to two factors – apart, of course, from Jill's diligence and expertise. The first was practical – it had been a 'dropping' summer, with pleasant warm sunshine interspersed regularly, with quite heavy rain: thus, no better weather for a West Country garden. The second factor was psychological, for Alec Conway sat on his patio in such good spirits that if he had been gazing out at a scrap yard, he would have seen some beauty in it. The reason for such joy, and the fact he was sitting sipping a glass of wine feeling totally relaxed – rare in itself – and at peace with the world, was simply that early that afternoon the New Age Travellers had finally moved on, thereby returning the Town Fields to the people of Brendon Combe. Also, they had been returned in tolerable order, the most unsightly evidence of their occupation being the blackened remains of a huge bonfire around which they had partied long into the night preceding their afternoon departure.

Conway also felt pleased with life because he had found out at that time via the highly reliable source of local news and gossip that was his wife, that, as a magistrate, much praise and thanks were already coming in his direction from relieved local residents who saw the recent actions of the bench as being the main reason why the Travellers had moved out. And the fact that the councillor had declared an interest and in consequence had not sat that morning, in no way abated the praise which came in his direction – praise which could be credit in the electoral bank, there being council elections the following May. For in the minds of many local folk, there was the belief that whilst Conway might not have sat that morning, it was he who orchestrated the actions of the bench, and the subsequent reactions of the Travellers.

The two magistrates that morning had, in accordance with their habitual practice – and the law – imposed penalty points and fines upon all the Travellers who were brought before them on the motoring offences. The fines had ranged from £60 to £450, with the Travellers being given seven days in which to pay. By that following Thursday afternoon, six days after the fines had been imposed, not a single pound had been paid, and before the afternoon was out, not a single Traveller remained in the Town Fields. Where they had gone, nobody knew, and equally, nobody was likely to enquire – including the local police. Some of their colleagues elsewhere would either have or be about to have, similar problems of course, and the local court was owed a considerable sum in unpaid fines. But such is life, reasoned the Brendon Combe constabulary, whilst the local population and, naturally, the local council felt an overwhelming sense of relief this seemingly intractable problem had been resolved at last.

"Yes," mused Alec Conway to himself, "it's been a most successful day."

"Alec." The councillor's reverie was shattered; Jill stood on the edge of the patio holding a cordless phone in her hand. "It's Colin Butler," said she. "Says he needs to speak to you urgently."

"Probably to tell me those blasted Travellers have gone. Thanks maid," said he, taking the phone from his wife, then slumping back down onto the patio chair.

"Hello, Colin, I reckon you're a happy man now our guests in the Town Fields have departed."

"I was until about an hour ago," rasped the works manager. "I've been down to have a close look at the Fields – to see if any real damage has been done. I've been on the phone to the Mayor, and the Chairman of Properties and Finance – I thought they should know first. But seeing as you're the senior member of the council in terms of years of service, I thought you should know as well. It's about the seats, Alec."

"What – the ones by the churchyard, especially the broken one; have you found out yet who does own them?"

153

"The ones by the churchyard?" The voice had a tone of bewilderment about it. "The ones by the churchyard?" repeated the works manager. "Oh, I'm with you Alec – no, no, not those. Hell no – I'm afraid they've gone to the bottom of the priority list, Alec; no I'm referring to the seats all around the Town Fields."

"What about them, Colin?" The question was asked fearfully, the councillor realising there was almost certainly going to be pain involved in the answer.

"Well, there aren't any."

"What – no seats. You mean the Travellers have nicked them – taken them with them wherever they've gone?"

"No, they've not done that. You know that bonfire last night – well the wood used to make it so big and bright, was the seats. They've burned the lot. With all the treatment the wood in those seats have had over the years, it's not surprising there were such huge flames coming from the bonfire – you could see it from all over town. I've also phoned Harold Newman – he's not sure if our insurance will cover such an act of arson. We could be faced with a bill for thousands to replace them. Sorry to bring you such news, Alec, but I thought you ought to know. Anyway, there's going to be an extraordinary meeting of the council next Tuesday to discuss what's to be done. They'll send out an agenda from the office tomorrow, Alec. Sorry to bring you such news. Good night."

The councillor stood as if turned to stone, not even returning a courteous 'good night' or 'thank you' to Butler. Slowly, he moved towards the back door of the house to return the telephone to its receiver. Just minutes before, he had felt pleased with life – especially his public one. Now he suddenly asked the question of that life which many had asked themselves over the years, the decades – 'surely there was a better way to live life than to concern himself with the vagaries, idiocies, selfishness and wantonness which characterised so much of human nature? Surely there was a better, less fraught path to follow?'

The answer to both questions, undoubtedly, was 'yes' – in theory, at least. Yet, he had never been a great one for theory. He liked doing things and knew that if he ceased to involve himself in the maelstrom that was local public life then, within a month, he would be bored out of his mind. He replaced the phone upon the receiver, returned to the patio, poured himself another glass of wine, and then sat once again gazing at the garden, his mind already wrestling with the problem of the Town Fields' seats – or, to be more accurate, the lack of them.

# XII

# The Rocks Below, the Sky Above

It was Myra's idea to start with. He was reasonably happy with life – or, at least, not unhappy – and certainly had no great desire to change his life or his way of living it, having a routine with which he was both familiar and reasonably satisfied. Myra, though – who almost invariably felt that other people's grass was greener – wanted a change, and wanted it desperately.

"All this traffic, noise, fumes, people. I've had enough of it," she had said. "Come on, let's get away from it all. Go down to Devon. It's glorious down there."

But he hadn't wanted to go. He was an architect and his business was flourishing. London was his future. He could have none in Devon – or, at least, none that he could see. But she had talked him round as she usually did.

"You can sell this business for a small fortune," she told him, "and then invest some of the money in a business, say, perhaps a shop or something like that, down in Devon. We would be able to make a good living down there and enjoy the fresh air, warm sun, golden sands and quiet, gentle life. And we could always visit London for a week or two occasionally, if we wished."

And she had convinced him that paradise awaited them both if they moved West, whilst the hectic London life would destroy them both eventually. So he sold his business for a handsome profit, invested some of it in a gift-shop in a traditionally picturesque fishing village on the north coast of Devon and they both kicked the London dust from their feet and moved West towards paradise promised.

After a few months his reservations about moving from his native London had completely disappeared. He grew to love Devon and the little village in which they lived. The soft, lilting accent of the villagers, the smell of the sea, the cooling dampness of the south-west wind, the towering cliffs, the peace and solitude, the brooding anger of the Atlantic that washed onto the local shores. All these things and more made this village a paradise for him. All his life he had lived in a maelstrom of noise, smells, bustle, ulcers, worry and had thought that there was no other path in life. And now he had found this. He was in love – with this village, with Devon itself. He would never leave it.

But Myra was different. Oh yes, she had talked him into going down to the West Country. When she had been there on holiday it seemed a glorious place to live. And she was fed up with London. Anyway, she liked moving around, seeing different places. And she felt that if Frank gave up his business in London and sold it at a great profit, then they could buy a summer business in Devon, close up in October and spend the winter months travelling the world, really seeing life and enjoying themselves. But somehow things had not worked out the way she had planned.

The first summer they were in the village things were all right. The local people were surprisingly friendly and helpful, contrary to various stories they had heard before living amongst them. The tourists, true to form, came to the quaint old village in their droves, took innumerable snap-shots, had a bumpy, and expensive, ride around the choppy bay in one of the fishing boats that hadn't bothered about catching fish for the last twenty years, and then came to the gift-shop just before the bus was about to leave for the next overnight stop. And they bought all manner of rubbish. Lumps of rock marked Devon, with a small lead seagull sitting on top, plaster of Paris pixies, toby jugs, cheap earrings, cups and saucers with local scenes painted on them – those and a thousand and one other items were duly gobbled up by the insatiable tourist appetite.

The profits at the end of that summer were colossal and Myra confidently looked forward to the globetrotting that the winter would bring. But Frank was a greatly changed man. For the first time in his life he was happy and content. He loved the village and never wanted to leave it, not even for a day. His excuses for staying in the place all winter were many and varied.

"We'll have to keep the shop open," he said. "We'll lose trade otherwise." He ignored the fact that during the winter months there were no more than half a dozen holidaymakers in the whole of the county. "If we leave the house empty it will get damp, cold and will deteriorate," was another excuse.

So Myra had to spend the winter in a lonely Devon coastal village which whilst in summer had a certain beauty and grandeur, had in winter a cold, damp dreariness – even desolation – about it. She pleaded, threatened, begged, but Frank would not shift from his castle, his newly-formed empire – and the Devonshire winter ran its course; successions of gales, the turbulent Atlantic doing its best to wash the village away, sheets of rain day after day, damp, heavy fog, black nights and sombre days. And the village held nothing in the way of entertainment. The pub that only opened when the landlord felt like it, and a fish and chip shop that, ironically, always seemed to be running out of fish, were the only places to go. The high cliffs destroyed good reception of television programmes and any storm that came along, and there seemed to be half a dozen each week, knocked out the electricity supply.

Frank spent the winter reading, sleeping, walking over the storm-ridden cliffs, and generally trying to pick up a way of life that he realised, deep down, he had always longed for. Myra spent the short, damp days and long, stormy nights in a constant state of frustration, anger and boredom seemingly with nothing to do but light smelly oil lamps when the erratic electricity supply failed, and mop up the copious quantities of water which seeped underneath the front door – from the Atlantic! How she longed to be back in London and the twenty-first century, wishing she had never set eyes on the saturated outpost that was the far South West of England. She made up her mind that come what may she would never spend another winter in this land of the lost.

The winter passed slowly but eventually the days began to get longer although not much drier. April arrived and with it the first tourists and, as before, the trickle became a flood. The cash register of the gift-shop could hardly cope and Myra thought happily that the profits this year, allied to the money they had in the bank and the large amount they would get for the gift-shop when they sold it, would mean they would be able to get back to London, buy a reasonably nice house – despite the ever escalating property prices – invest some of the money in some business or other, be able to live in semi-retirement and travel the world, on and off, for the rest of their lives. Of course, there was Frank's stubbornness to overcome. But she would be able to handle that all right. And anyway, after having spent a hellish winter in this godforsaken spot he'd probably be just as anxious as her to spend the short days back in civilisation. And once they were out of Devon, they wouldn't be coming back – she'd see to that.

The summer passed. Crowded August gave way to sunny September and then the shorter, crisper days of October – and the last tourists climbed aboard their buses, or clambered into their long suffering cars and took the long road back to their factories, offices and Job Centres. And Myra told Frank that it was time they also packed their bags, sold out and made once more for the asphalt civilisation that was London.

"We've made sufficient here in two years to live like Lords. And just think what this place will fetch now. Along with what we have in the bank, well, we could almost retire."

But Frank shook his head. "I'm not leaving here, Myra," he said softly. "Not now or ever. For the first time in my life I am really happy. I've found everything that I ever wanted from life in this place. Contentment, a sense of purpose, a sense of values. I'm sorry my love, but I just cannot leave here. I couldn't be happy anywhere else."

It was then that Myra had delivered her ultimatum. Eyeing him angrily, almost viciously, her voice cold as ice, she said; "I'm telling you this Frank, and I mean it. I'm not spending one more winter in this damned place. In fact, I'm not spending another week here, now or ever. If you won't leave here with me then I'll leave on my own. I've got some money in the bank in my own name so I won't starve, don't worry about that. But I mean what I say. If you refuse to take me away from this place, then I'm leaving on my own." She paused and then added in a hard, almost mocking tone of voice, "I'll leave you Frank – reluctantly, true, but as I've just said, if you won't come with me, I'll go on my own."

He had laughed and gone for a walk along the cliffs. She wouldn't leave him. She didn't have enough money to do that. Myra had expensive tastes and she needed what they had in the bank to indulge them. And he laughed again when she repeated her threat the following day, and the day after. But he stopped laughing on the fourth day when he arrived home after a long walk over the cliffs to the north and found her note:

> *I've gone and I will not be coming back;*
> *you will hear from my solicitor.*
> *Myra*

That was all it said.

That he was taken aback there was no doubt. The car was in the garage so she must have caught the noon bus out of the village, for that was the only one between nine in the morning and four in the afternoon. He hadn't left until about half-past ten and was back again at half-past three. Clearly she had packed for her short term needs without him knowing it, and not long after he had left the house, she must have taken her suitcase and caught the bus. He never thought she had it in her. But then, the world was full of surprises. However, after looking about the house he was convinced she'd not be gone for long. For the bulk of her clothes and personal possessions were still there – although her jewellery, which was quite valuable, had gone – and the money she had in the bank would not last her long. There was a fair sum in their business account, of course, but she would not be able to access that, even though it was a joint account, for the only cheque book was with their accountants, temporarily, their books being audited. As to the threat regarding her solicitor, whilst it had made him feel a touch uneasy, he did not really feel she would instruct him. No, when her cash had gone, she would probably do what he would expect of her – come back, albeit somewhat unwillingly, and spend their money, and try to organise him as she had in the past.

The weeks passed, however, and turned into months; autumn became winter – but still she had not returned, nor had she sent for her possessions, or set her solicitors on the case. In fact, he'd not heard a word from her, and knew not where she was living, or anything else about her, and he didn't really care, either.

He was completely alone – but not lonely, not in the slightest. He enjoyed solitude, the peace, the absence of pressures that had always seemed to be around him before. And for the first time in his life he saw things really clearly. He realised now that he had always been basically unhappy with Myra and that he didn't want her to come back – in fact, he never wanted to see her again. It was only now that she was gone he really discovered how much she had controlled his life. She had always been pushing him, relentlessly, without ceasing. She had pushed him to make money, and more money, to build up successful businesses, to desert his principles and basic honesty and decency just so that he would be able to keep with the leaders in the rat-race of life. And she spent the money he made and pushed and organised him in such a way that he didn't really have a mind of his own. For years he had been the puppet and she had pulled the strings. And he had only just realised it – that was the tragedy of it all. He had been a good meal ticket for Myra and she had known how to make use of him. But not any more. He had found happiness at last and was damned sure that he wasn't going to lose it now.

Soon spring came once again, but still no word from Myra. Summer arrived and the tourists with it; then it went and they along with it – but leaving a lot of their money in Frank's cash register. And then, damp, cold winter once more when Frank would spend his time reading, sleeping perhaps just sitting and thinking. On a sunny day he would walk across the cliffs. Sometimes he went southwards towards the lonely light-house on the headland. Other times, north towards the little fishing village of Bolton Cove where he would have a pint or two in the local and then go up to the railway station and watch the trains coming and going on the branch line – coming from a life which he had almost forgotten, to a kind of Eden, and then, reluctantly turning around and making their way back to the jungle once more. Then he would turn away and make for home. For that's what it was to him now. The first and only real home that he had ever had, and he treasured it as he had treasured nothing else in the whole of his life.

He loved the little village – the peace, the simplicity, the sanity, the people. And the locals liked and respected him, always making him feel welcome when he dropped into the village pub for a pint or two. But his visits were not very frequent. He preferred the company of his own thoughts; the taste of salt air meant more to him than the taste of beer; the sound of gulls overhead made better music to him than the harsh grating of voices. He felt more at home amidst the wild loneliness and splendour of the cliffs than amidst the warm cosiness of the village inn. He had become what the world terms a 'recluse', perhaps even a hermit. But the world spits out the word with either contempt or incomprehension – perhaps at times even arrogant superiority – not knowing, or understanding, what it is missing. For the first time in his life Frank felt like a winner and he loved every second of it. And he was determined of one thing – come what may, he was never going to be a loser again.

Winter turned into spring and spring to summer, once again, and still he heard no word from Myra. When she first went away he thought that about three months would be her limit. He had expected her to come back broke and take over where she had left off. But she had not returned, nor had she sent for her things, or any part of them. She hadn't even written to him. Not a word of any kind from her in two years. Possibly even more relevantly, he had received nothing from a solicitor saying she wanted a divorce, or cash settlement, or anything of that nature.

It was very strange; what was she doing? More importantly, how was she living? Who was keeping her? Her parents had died years before. She hadn't a single friend in the world, that he knew of, and none of her relatives were close to her. She could have got a job, or course, but he couldn't see her getting any work which would bring her anything more than a basic living. She had no profession, no real training at all when it came to work. Perhaps she had found another meal ticket. After all, she was an attractive woman and she had always possessed the knack of latching on to money. At that very moment she was probably soothing the troubled brow of some wealthy executive in some penthouse or other, and charging excessively for the service. Oh yes, Myra would look after herself all right, there was no doubt about that. Just as long as she stayed in the penthouse and didn't come back to Devon again, that was all he asked. But as time went on, Frank thought less and less about her and eventually she became just a vague memory in some recess of his mind; eventually he could scarce remember a life which didn't contain the sea, the cliffs, the gulls, the loneliness and rural wildness of Devon.

Month followed month and season followed season, and soon more than five years had passed since Myra had left him. It was now late November and everything was wet and sombre with a light drizzle drifting in from the grey Atlantic, carried on a light south-westerly wind. Frank came in from the garden where he had been patiently trimming the low bank which ran down to the road in front of the house and shop. The early winter darkness was beginning to fall, so he turned on the lights and lit the log fire in the grate. After a meal of stew, which he considered his speciality, he settled down in front of the roaring fire with a book. Few pages had been turned over however, before the book fell from his limp fingers and he drifted into a warm contented sleep. His rest was short-lived for he was soon awakened by a loud banging at the door. He sat still for a few seconds collecting his thoughts but at the sound of fresh banging he wearily got up and made for the door. He opened it and looked out into the blackness. The light from the room fell upon two uniformed figures. The elder looking of the two spoke first.

"Mr Frank Marshall?"

Frank nodded and muttered; "Yes, that's right. What's the trouble?"

"Do you think we could come in sir, please?"

"Yes, of course," said Frank, with the urgency of a man who had just realised that he had forgotten his manners. The two men walked into the warm room and Frank closed the door behind them, a puzzled look on his face.

"We'd better introduce ourselves sir. I'm Sergeant Collins of Devon and Cornwall Police and this is Constable Trewin. We feel that you might be able to help us sir, if you'd be good enough to answer a few questions."

"Yes, of course," replied Frank, a worried look on his features now.

"I understand that your wife has not lived here with you for some time, sir. How long ago did she leave?"

"About five years ago. Perhaps a little more."

"Have you any idea where she is now, sir?"

"No idea at all. I haven't seen her since the day she left me. Haven't heard from her. She could be dead for all I know."

"She could indeed, sir." The sergeant looked at him coldy. "To be quite honest, we think she is."

Frank jerked his head up, an expression of shock on his face.

"The remains of a woman's body were recovered from the face of the cliffs today, sir," continued the sergeant in a level, business-like tone of voice. "A rock climber was scaling the face of the cliffs to the north of here, near Bolton Cove, when he came upon this decomposed body in a rock cleft about halfway down. When he got to the top he contacted us and, of course, we brought the body to the top. Obviously it was impossible to identify the woman, but caught up in the cleft along with the body, were a handbag and a suitcase. We found the name of Mrs Myra Marshall, and this address, written inside, sir."

"My God," muttered Frank, a look of sheer horror on his face. "It doesn't seem possible." He paused, still trying to absorb the news. "How long do you think her body has been there?" he continued.

"Hard to say without a pathologist's examination. But we think between four and five years. That would roughly tie in with when she left you, sir, wouldn't it?"

"Yes, I suppose it would," said Frank, nodding. "The day she went she left a note on the table saying she was off and wouldn't be back. When I read it, I assumed that she caught the morning bus out of the village. Instead, she must have walked along the cliffs with the intention of catching a train at Bolton Cove. Somehow she must have fallen over the edge." He paused and shook his head in disbelief. "It just doesn't seem possible. I've walked over those cliffs scores of times since then. To think that she'd been lying there all this time and I've been walking along only a few yards from her. It doesn't make sense, does it? Quite astounding."

The sergeant didn't answer his question. Instead he beckoned to the constable and turned again to Frank.

"I'm afraid we shall have to ask you to make a statement, sir. The constable will take it down now if it's all right with you?"

"Yes, yes, I understand."

Frank told them everything he knew and the constable put it all down. When they had finished, the two uniformed men got up from the armchairs in which they had been sitting, and moved for the door.

"Thank you very much, sir," said the sergeant efficiently. "You will of course, be informed of the time of the inquest and of any other developments. We'd be most obliged if you would stay in the village for the next few days. There might be some further questions that we shall need to ask you."

"I understand, Sergeant. I never go very far anyway."

The two policemen walked out of the door. "Goodnight, sir," they chorused together.

"Goodnight."

Frank shut the door behind them and walked unsteadily to his armchair beside the fire. No wonder Myra hadn't written to him all those years. She had been lying out there on the cliffs – dead. He sat upright and looked into the fire. The news had shocked him, of course. But deep down it hadn't really upset him. It should have. After all, he had loved Myra when he had married her all those years before and their life together had not been so bad really. But over these last few years he had grown used to living alone and now wanted no other way of life. If he was honest with himself, he wasn't upset, he was glad. His life of seclusion was safe now for all time.

But a chilling thought struck him. The sergeant's eyes had been cold and accusing. He had looked at Frank in the same way as he would look at a guilty man. Surely he and the rest of the police didn't suspect him of anything. They couldn't suspect him of . . . God no, not that, surely. But they did. He had seen it in the sergeant's face and in the constable's – they thought that he had pushed Myra over the side of the cliff. But he hadn't. He hadn't. Of course, he couldn't prove it – but then, neither could they. No, they couldn't touch him. Why the hell was he panicking like this? The inquest would clear him of all blame and then he would be able to carry on as before. Nothing had changed. Nothing would change.

But Frank was wrong. Things had changed – and people also. When he walked to the village general store next day everybody seemed to try to avoid him. They crossed the road as he came towards them, or turned their heads and looked in the opposite direction. If he spoke to them, they returned a terse greeting and gathered in little groups and talked secretively together, gazing at him somewhat malevolently all the time. And Frank could imagine just what they were saying. "Murdered his wife, he did. Pushed her over a cliff. They ought to lock him up" – and all the time the long, cold, silent stares from people who only a few days before had treated him as one of them, had talked pleasantly to him, liked him and respected him. But the inquest would sort things out. When the coroner told everybody that he was not to blame for anything then things would be different – it would be just like old times again.

But the coroner didn't say that. As Frank sat in the cold courtroom in Barnstaple he saw the same bleak accusing look in the coroner's eyes as he saw in everybody else's. And he came under the lash of the worthy man's tongue also. Why had he not reported his wife missing? If she was leaving him where was the note she was supposed to have left? Why was she leaving him anyway and where was she going? He didn't appear to be a man who was unduly upset at the death of his wife. Why not? A hundred and one searching, accusing questions came at him, each one asked in a tone of voice that seemed to say, "You're guilty all right. If only we could prove it." But they couldn't prove it and Frank knew it as well as the coroner. The worthy man returned an open verdict and asked to be informed if the police made any further progress in their investigations. Frank left the courtroom with the finger of accusation pointing at him from all sides.

The happenings of the inquest were relayed to one and all by the villagers who had made the trip to Barnstaple to see that justice was done. Their stories grew in length, became exaggerated, twisted and before long Frank's name was listed in the company of Crippen, Christie, and the Yorkshire Ripper. He became feared, ostracised, even hated by the whole village; life became barren, lonely and futile for him.

He had always kept largely to himself in the village but he had always enjoyed the friendship and respect that he had grown to expect from the locals. Now all around him was hatred, silence and suspicion. Soon life in general became impossible. The milkman stopped calling each morning, without giving any explanation. The village store always seemed to run out of what he wanted. The landlord of the village inn told him that he wasn't welcome in his bar. The coal-man refused to deliver coal to him, the baker, bread, the butcher, meat. He was pushed back into his little shop and house like a mouse was pushed into a hole. And he didn't understand it. None of it. He had done no harm to anyone. Not to Myra. Not to anyone in the village. But he had been tried and found guilty in the Court of Public Opinion and Vicious Gossip. He had been sentenced to be destroyed. There was no appeal, no reprieve. Frank Marshall was a condemned man and there was no way out.

As the winter went on the persecution increased. One morning he found his picturesque garden completely destroyed – his rose bushes cut to pieces, his neat wooden seats smashed up, his smooth lawns desecrated by a turning fork. One afternoon, while he was out for a walk, somebody got into the shop and smashed the place to pieces. Antiques, curios, gifts, the lot. He began to realise that he had no chance. The villagers were determined to get him out and his will to fight them was diminished. He was living in a world of suspicion, hatred and violence. He wanted no part of it. He wanted to find that world of contentment again. The contentment which had been his for well over five years. But it was gone from this place now and would never return.

Frank sold his shop and house. He sold it lock, stock and barrel. He wanted no part of it any more, no part of this village, no part of Devon, or, indeed, the wider South West. Where he was going to go he didn't really know – nor did he care. Life seemed to have little meaning.

The battered taxi came for his luggage and he soon loaded it aboard. He was going to ride with it to the station at Bolton Cove, but then changed his mind. He would walk along the cliffs as he had done so many times before. His last walk. He sent the taxi on its way and began to walk along the high, barren cliffs. He walked slowly, mechanically, like a robot. His mind was so confused, it was incapable of any sound, logical thought. There was just the feel of the wind against his face, the roar of the sea in his ears and despair in his heart. He walked like a man in the middle of a nightmare from which he would never awake.

After a while he stopped and moved towards the edge of the cliff. He stopped on the brink and looked down the sheer face of it to the black rocks and frothing sea below. At that moment he knew Myra had won. She had succeeded in death where she had failed in life – she had made him leave the place that he had grown to love, for – for what? He stood looking down at the cauldron of rock and water. His eyes were glazed, his brain and body numb. But he hadn't left Devon yet had he? After all, wasn't that glorious county all around him. Anyway why should Myra win after all? She had nearly always won in life – why should she win in death as well? Down there was a new world, a world without Myra, without enemies, without problems, without despair. All he had to do to join that world was to jump. Yes, that's all he had to do – jump.

He swayed on the edge of the cliff, still looking down. "Jump you fool," he said to himself. "For once in your life make a

168

decision and stick to it." But he had made a mess of many things in life – what if he made a mess of this as well?

What if there was no new world down there? What if there was only oblivion? The sea seemed to mock him as he stood gazing morosely down at it. It seemed to see him as the coward he was. Tears came into his eyes and he turned away and began to stumble along the cliff towards the station. The new world was only for the brave – he was condemned to live in the old . . .

h

# XIII

# Of Men and Marrows

Will Dobson put down his watering can and looked proudly at his marrow. He sighed with pleasure. He was seventy-one years old and had been growing marrows for more years than he could remember, but never one like this. It was simply magnificent. A real beauty. Of course, they could grow them even bigger than this up the country, but then they had just the right type of soil and climate up there. The heavy Devon soil, allied to a very wet climate, made the growing of prize marrows a very difficult task indeed, but old Will reckoned that, despite the handicaps imposed by soil and weather, he could grow a marrow that would hold its own with most of the ones up the line and that would make anything grown locally look like a turnip by comparison. Anyway, if nothing else, he would make that Arthur Crowley look the big-headed fool he was, that was for sure. He had worked for many, many months to put that damned upstart in his place, but he would not have to wait much longer. The show was less than a fortnight away.

His feud with Arthur Crowley had begun the best part of twelve months before, not long after the previous year's show in fact. Will was in the saloon bar of the Whistler's Arms having his nightly pint or two of bitter, and playing dominoes. The door opened, a stranger entered and Will took a dislike to him as soon as he saw him. Before very long most people in the pub felt the same way. The stranger, about forty or perhaps a little younger, introduced himself as Arthur Crowley and said that he had just moved into the village from some place in the Midlands, although most of this was already known. The news that a new family – a man, woman and two kids – had moved into Willow Cottage had gone around the tight little village in less than an hour. The stranger drank only whisky, not beer like most of the regulars, and being a conservative bunch, this put the locals off to begin with. Then the tall, well-built Midlander began to lecture the regulars, who previously had all been engrossed in quiet, friendly conversation, or playing dominoes and darts, about the shortcomings and deficiencies of their charming village.

Old Percy Hartland, the landlord of the Whistler's Arms for thirty-five years and more, also came under the lash of the stranger's tongue. He was told that his pub was the same as the village, as a whole – old-fashioned, scruffy, inhospitable and lacking in all modern amenities. Poor old Percy really objected to this and nearly had a seizure. He would surely have tried to take a swing at the stranger had not Jim Barker rushed to the bar and calmed the old chap down. Still keeping an eye on the bristling Percy and also seeing the anger of the other villagers, he turned to the stranger and eyed him coldly, his anger held in check by a gigantic will-power.

"I'll tell you something mate, for nothing," he said steadily, his eyes fixed upon the stranger. "We're easy going, good tempered people here. We welcome strangers to come and live here if they wish. But if they do then we expect them to abide by the way of life here. A fair number have moved here in recent times, with all the new houses and so forth and most are as good as gold and happy with life here. Those, though, who aren't, can leave and move off somewhere else – go to hell if they like. Now I'm telling you this, and I'm telling you straight. If you come in here saying the things you've just said – well, next time you'll be on your back and even if I don't put you there, there are plenty others who will. Anyway, I don't know what you've got to shout about so much. I worked up in the Midlands for a few months a couple of years ago. I was out of work down here so I went up there and got a job in a factory. Never again though. Filthiest place I ever lived

171

in all my life. And the people were the most unfriendly I ever came across. A horrible place all round. No wonder they call it the Black Country."

It was the newcomer's turn to be angry now. "What the hell are you talking about?" he stormed. "There's nothing wrong with the Midlands, not in any field you care to mention. Hub of the nation it is. Backbone of the country. Not like this place. Let's be honest, if the south-west disappeared off the map – the face of the earth – who would miss it? Nobody except perhaps for a few holidaymakers and they would soon learn that they could have a better holiday abroad – and a good deal cheaper as well. It would just mean that the country would have less dole money to pay out, that's all. But if the Midlands disappeared, the country would go bankrupt, wouldn't it? Stands to reason. Seventy-five per cent of all the nation's industry's there, isn't it? No, compared with the Midlands the south-west is backward and produces little of any value. As to this village, well . . ." He finished with a shrug of his shoulders and a sardonic laugh.

Will Dobson had listened to all of this from his seat in the corner, and hadn't uttered a word. He was an even-tempered man. In fact, he'd never been known to really lose his temper in the whole of his life, but he felt the anger rising inside himself now.

"Look here, pal," he said, his voice level and unemotional, despite the anger he felt. "If it's so bloody handsome up there why don't you pack your things and take yourself out of here and go back there. It would give us some peace if nothing else. And not only that – it would leave a house vacant for some decent, friendly folk who might want to live here, instead of an ignorant troublemaker like yourself. A home possibly for some local folk who cannot afford to buy now because of the way you incomers keep forcing up the prices."

The regulars in the pub looked at Will with something approaching amazement on their faces. Most of them had known him all or most of their lives, which in many cases went back a long, long time, but none of them had ever heard him talk so forthrightly and angrily before. The newcomer was flushed with anger and for a minute looked as if he was going to go over to the corner and lay into old Will. He must have thought better of it, however, for he picked up his whisky – his fourth in a very short time – and downed what was left of it in one gulp and then turned to Will.

"I wouldn't stay in this lousy village one minute unless I had to," he said, his anger oozing from every pore. "The firm I work for has bought the cottage I'm living in and as long as I work for this firm I'll be living in the cottage. But if I had known where the cottage was situated I would never have agreed to come down here. But still, I'll have the last laugh. I'm taking over as assistant manager of a factory in Plymouth, so I'll have a lot of you Devon yokels working for me, won't I?" He said the words with real venom and there were mutterings from some of the younger men in the pub about 'doing him over' and, 'teaching the ignorant bugger a lesson' and so on. Crowley, though, still wasn't quite finished.

"Of course," he continued, "it just goes to prove the truth of what I say. After all, I've had to come three hundred miles to supervise you. You cannot hack it on your own, any of you. You can't do anything properly. It doesn't matter what activity you partake in, you'd take a hammering from us. No matter whether it's work, or football, or rugby or cricket, or any sport at all, or even basic intelligence for that matter, we'd leave you standing the lot of you." He finished with a self-satisfied smile and began to move towards the door.

"Just a minute," said Will.

The stranger stopped and looked towards him.

"How about gardening?" asked the local man, quietly.

"What do you mean?" replied the stranger, a puzzled look on his face.

"Well, you said that you could leave us standing at anything we cared to mention, or words to that effect anyway. So what about gardening? Do you reckon you could leave us standing at that as well?" Will's voice was quiet, but deadly serious and he appeared to deflate the stranger somewhat. Crowley soon recovered himself however, and, although he suspected a trap, immediately shot back the answer that was expected of him.

"Certainly I could. Give me a while to get myself organised and I'll produce the best garden in the village. I used to do a lot of gardening back home. Used to win prizes in the local shows and all. There's not much you can tell me about gardening." The Midlander had fully recovered himself and was as arrogant as ever.

Old Will took a sip from his pint and gazed at him, a shrewd look in his eyes.

"Ever grown marrows?" he asked casually, and as soon as he said that, it dawned on all the regulars exactly what he was playing at. For Will was a good gardener in every sense. No matter what he grew, it was usually better than anybody else grew. His marrows however were his crowning glory and they were always far, far bigger and better than those produced by others. This was proved by the fact that for the last fifteen years, he had always carried off the cup for the best marrow at the local show. A few years earlier he used to have some fairly keen competition, but his rivals got so fed up with being beaten every year that they decided they were pursuing a hopeless cause and thus gave it up, leaving Will's magnificent marrow as the only entry in that section of the show for the last three years. But the stranger wasn't to know this and therefore seemed certain to fall into the trap that old Will baited for him. He didn't let them down.

"Yes, 'course I've grown marrows," he replied briskly. "Grown ones that would make yours look like gooseberries I shouldn't wonder. Why do you ask anyway?"

The stranger was about to fall and everybody in the pub knew it. If he hadn't been so full of his own importance he would have noticed the sly grins around him.

"Well," said Will, taking another sip from his pint, "if you grow marrows and grow them as well as you say you do, I was thinking that perhaps you would like to enter one in the local show next year. I grow marrows myself. In fact I've taken the cup at the show, in the marrow section, for the last fifteen years. But then if you're as good at growing them as you say you are, well you won't have a lot of trouble in beating me and carrying off the cup will you?" Old Will picked up his pint again and waited for the stranger's reaction.

Crowley looked around himself a touch nervously and felt his face flush. He suddenly realised that these damned locals had laid a trap for him and he had fallen into it head first. If he refused the challenge now he'd be the laughing stock of the village. He was a man who didn't give a damn about people disliking him, but he couldn't stand people laughing at him. There was only one possible reply, and he went ahead and gave it.

"Good idea," he said, trying to sound patronising. "I'll most certainly enter a marrow next year and show you what a real marrow looks like. I'd like to enter in all the other vegetable sections as well, but unfortunately my work will occupy my time to such an extent that I won't have the spare time to attend to it. Not like you retired chaps with nothing else to do you know." He reached for his raincoat behind the bar door and then swung around with sudden inspiration. "Tell you what," he said. "How about us having a little wager on the result of this marrow contest. Say, fifty pounds?" He reached for his wallet and took some notes from a wad that bulged out the inside.

Old Will was a bit taken aback as were the rest of the locals. This upstart certainly had some nerve, there were no two ways about that.

"Yes, all right," muttered Will. "I've not got it on me at present mind you – never carry a lot of cash." He didn't say what he thought – that to him fifty quid was a lot of money. "We'll leave it with the landlord," said the stranger, "and the night of the show next year, the winner will be able to claim them both. I'll trust you to put your fifty with him in the next few days. Look after it safely, Landlord," he said as he handed the notes over. "I'm looking forward to having a very, very good night out on that hundred pounds. Good night everybody."

The stranger waved his hand flamboyantly and walked to the door. He felt quite pleased with himself. He had got himself into a trap but had turned the situation to his own advantage and had emerged from the fracas the moral winner. But then so he should, or so he felt. After all, he was dealing with a bunch of peasants. He felt almost sorry for them in a way.

And behind him, in the Whistler's Arms, he left spluttering anger. In much earlier times the stranger would have been chased out of the village or perhaps, if luck were against him, put into stocks on the village green. But these days were different. The age of psychology, the age of village vegetable shows. Percy Hartland, the landlord, summed up everybody's feelings. "Will," he said quietly, "if you give that bloke the hammering he deserves, with your marrow next year, I'll give you more beer than you can drink in six months. Grow the biggest marrow you've ever grown in your life and show that damned bugger up for the big-mouthed fool he is."

There were cries of "Here, here" from all over the pub and many other dark mutterings about the stranger's parents.

Old Will was heard to say, "I'll do my best. I'll do my best, lads." But he had a strange feeling of foreboding as he went home that night.

The cold winter came and went, the short days became longer and spring turned into summer. Old Will tended his marrow with loving care. He spent so much time on his marrow in fact, that the rest of his garden suffered from lack of attention. The garden still looked quite good and the flowers and vegetables were of quite a high standard, but nowhere near that which he usually achieved. But Will wasn't worried. His marrow was the best that he had ever grown and that was the main thing. Crowley would slink away to the nearest hole when he saw it and serve him right, big-headed, big-mouthed devil. And he hadn't improved any.

The stranger, for that's what he was and that's what he would always be the way he carried on, had been shouting his mouth off in the Whistler's Arms only the other night telling Will that he didn't stand a chance and that he ought to buy a coloured vase or something to fill the space where the cup had stood for the last fifteen years. And, although he didn't show it, it secretly angered Will, this arrogance from the newcomer; thus the success of his marrow became the focal point of his life. Some nights he was unable to sleep until he had been up to the garden and seen how the mighty vegetable, his pride and joy, was progressing.

The whole village knew of his feud with Crowley and were all on his side. For nobody liked the stranger or his wife and their children. It turned out that they were tarred with the same brush as their father. His wife looked down on all her neighbours and their two kids tried to bully the local children. So Will's marrow became the one hope of putting the strangers well and truly in their place and Will was not allowed to forget it. People asked after the state of his marrow, who didn't really know a marrow from a broad bean. Young and old men and women, children, even the vicar – who really shouldn't have taken sides – all came round to wish him luck, many saying that it would be a great pity if that nasty Mr Crowley were to win first prize and many others saying much the same thing in much stronger terms. So Will Dobson and his prize marrow were the hope and possible salvation of the village and he promised them that he wouldn't let them down – but he still had that feeling of foreboding.

The time was passing rapidly and old Will woke up one sunny morning after the most terrible nightmares, all peopled by giant marrows and giant Crowleys – and realised it was the morning of the local show. He was far too excited and nervous to have any breakfast. Instead he made immediately for his marrow and gave it a final grooming before taking it down to the village hall. He had no time to waste as everything had to be entered and properly staged by half-past nine. Still, Jim Barker dropped in as he had promised and helped the older man down the road with his giant exhibit to the sound of a hundred "good-lucks" from various people who were passing or looking out of their windows.

They reached the village hall and, with the help of scores of willing hands, soon had the monster properly staged. And it was only then, as people shook his hand and patted him on the back that he realised how deep was the feeling against Crowley. Most people seemed to positively hate him. Will was a mild-tempered man and didn't really hate the fellow. But he definitely disliked him and certainly wanted to teach him a lesson he wouldn't forget. And surely this magnificent marrow, that lay in front of them for the world to see, was unbeatable. Surely it was. Jim Barker seemed to read the old man's thoughts.

"He'll never beat that one, Will," he said, putting his arm

around the old fellow's shoulders. "You'll put our Midland friend in his place today, and no mistake." Jim looked up and laughed loudly. "Talk of the devil and here he comes," he said, pointing to the figure of Crowley who had just come in the door. He was followed by his two young sons who were pulling a largish trolley with a crate on board. The Midlander approached the knot of men around Will's marrow, with a wide grin on his face. As soon as he saw the grin, Will had a feeling that disaster was about to strike.

"Good morning all," he said cockily. He peered over Will's shoulder at the marrow lying in solitary state on the table. He started to laugh and a most unpleasant laugh it was. "Call that a marrow?" he said sarcastically. "Good God, I've grown potatoes bigger than that. If you want to see a marrow, look at this." The two sweating youngsters had just arrived with the trolley and packing case, which was covered by a blanket.

Crowley pulled aside the blanket and stood back so that the onlookers could see the contents of the crate. There was stunned silence, disturbed only by Will who was heard to mutter "Good God." For the crate contained the largest marrow any of them had ever seen. It was huge, absolutely gigantic. About half as big again as Will's.

The old man was shattered, and he went home a broken man. He wouldn't have minded if he had been just beaten. But this was an annihilation. His was like to toy beside Crowley's. It was the most humiliating moment of his life. That he lost a precious fifty pounds was the least of his concerns. The fact was he'd let the whole village down. Hadn't they all relied on him to put the arrogant stranger in his place and hadn't he more or less promised that he would do so. Now he'd let them down. And now Crowley would be even worse than before – and it was all his fault. The old man took his head in his hands and cried like a new born baby. At that moment the world seemed an awful place in which to live.

And Crowley did become worse than before and his wife and kids also. He seemed to spend more and more time in the Whistler's Arms boasting and taunting the locals. And all spirit seemed to have left the local lads and rather than stand up to the

Midlander they avoided him wherever he went and when he went into the Whistler's Arms they would all down their pints and leave. Poor old Percy Hartland's business gradually went to pieces. And old Will was rarely seen outside his own door and come to that, people didn't particularly want to see him. For they felt, very unfairly, that he had let them down. If only he had grown a decent sized marrow, instead of the tiny thing he had produced, then they would have been able to put the stranger in his place. But Will had humiliated them, humiliated the whole village and this accursed fellow was laughing at them, enjoying every minute of it. They didn't seem to realise that Will's marrow was the biggest that he had ever grown in his life. But he couldn't compete with the monster that Crowley had produced. Nobody could. It was a mystery how he ever grew one that size in the soil and climate that was Devon's.

The old man felt that his garden had let him down. But he had no other hobby so he still pottered about pulling weeds and growing vegetables and flowers like he always did. Due more to the force of habit than any other reason, he began to grow another marrow, and the following spring and summer he tended his plot with his usual meticulous care. But there seemed little purpose in it all. He couldn't possibly show any of it, not after the fool he had made of himself – and everybody else for that matter – the previous year; and Crowley, just to make matters even worse, had been going around saying that good though his prize-winning marrow was, it was small compared to the one that he would be putting in the show this year. "Not one of my best ones last year," he would say to anybody who couldn't avoid him. "This year I'll have one that will be large enough to live in."

He probably will too, reckoned the thoroughly dejected and defeated Will. Still, his would be the one and only entry. No entry from Will Dobson for the first time in . . . Will gave up trying to work out how many years it was. Jim Barker, still a good friend, came around and tried to persuade Will to enter his marrow this year. "You've got a fair to middling marrow out there Will," said the younger man kindly. "You never know, Crowley's might not be as good as he tells everybody it is."

"It was last year," said Will without spirit, and Jim, seeing that his task was hopeless, left the old man to brood alone.

There were only two days left before the show. Old Will was standing in the middle of his garden making the painful discovery that he had just run out of baccy for his pipe. He was lost without his smoke, so he went indoors, got his coat and sauntered off towards the shop belonging to Phil Pearce, down at the end of the village.

It was a nice day, sunny, with a cool breeze and Will was quite enjoying his little stroll. The trouble with him, and he was just beginning to realise it, was that he didn't get out enough. He spent too much time in his garden. Better for it if he went down to the Whistler's Arms a bit more, like he used to. Perhaps he would start going back there again. But the trouble was that he still felt kind of guilty. Silly really, but that's how it was.

He came out of his deep thoughts when up ahead he saw a delivery lorry parked outside Willow Cottage, the home of the Crowleys. As he got nearer, he saw that it was the one that Johnny Marker drove. Johnny's father, Bert, had been a good friend of Will's. Died of cancer a couple of years back had poor old Bert. A right case was Johnny. Liked the women and the beer – but a nice lad really. Will had always found him all right, anyway. As Will drew level with the lorry he saw Johnny mucking about in the back. "Hello there, Mr Dobson," Johnny shouted as he saw his father's old mate looking in the back of the lorry.

"Morning Johnny. How's it going then – all right?"

"It would be Mr Dobson, if I didn't have to unload this crate. Delivery for your old mate 'Lord' Crowley. But they've stacked it right on top of a whole pile of rubbish up the front here and I don't know how I'm going to get it down. Can't seem to get in there to get at it – if you see what I mean!"

"Can I give you a hand in any way?" volunteered Will, obligingly. He was still fairly fit for a man of his age and reckoned that he could easily manage one side of the packing case if the young man got hold of the other.

"Well perhaps you could, Mr Dobson. Thanks very much. If you could just help me to manoeuvre it a bit and then lift it down.

180

It's not particularly heavy really. Just very awkward."

Will scrambled into the back of the lorry and joined the driver, who was standing beside a heap of crates and parcels at the front. The offending crate was at the top and took quite a bit of reaching. Still, after much stretching and groaning they managed to manoeuvre the crate so that they could get a good grip on it. They then pulled it from the top of the pile and began to lower it. All would have gone well if Johnny hadn't stepped backwards. But step backwards he did and his foot found a piece of smooth wood and before he knew where he was he had lost his balance – and also his grip upon the crate. It fell heavily with a resounding crash and there was nothing that Will could do about it. He rushed forward to see if the prostrate Johnny was all right, but the young man said nothing. Instead he just lay on the floor and pointed at the partially disintegrated crate that was straight in front of him. Will turned and followed the line of his finger. And there, peeping out from the mass of broken wood, labels and straw, was the end of what could only be – a marrow?

Johnny jumped to his feet and rushed forward. Within seconds he had cleared away the debris revealing the most superb marrow that Will had ever set eyes upon. It was even bigger than Crowley's giant of the year before.

"Why the lousy bugger. The lousy crooked bugger." The words came from Johnny's lips before Will could say anything. He had sized up the situation quicker than his older friend. "No wonder he beat you last year, Mr Dobson. He's importing the damned things. He's not growing them at all. But he's finished now. I'll see to that. You stay here, I'm going to fetch Jerry Lawton."

Johnny disappeared up the road at a quick trot in search of the Secretary of the Show, leaving Will staring down at the gigantic marrow in amazement. He just could not believe it. It couldn't be true. Crowley was a big-mouth and the easiest man to dislike Will had ever met, but he had always thought him to be honest. Surely there was a mix-up somewhere.

The old man was still standing staring at the marrow that seemed almost like a figment of his imagination, when Johnny arrived back with Lawton. Jerry always had a week's holiday during show time because there was always too much to see to and Johnny had had little difficulty in finding him fussing around in the village hall.

The secretary looked at the vast vegetable lying on the floor of Johnny's lorry. He said that it looked suspicious but the only way to get a clear picture of the situation was to have a look in Crowley's garden. Being a former army officer Jerry always ran the show like a military operation and he felt that it was time to invade the Crowley property, and as Secretary of the Show, he had a perfect right to go into Crowley's garden, or anybody else's for that matter, if he suspected any jiggery-pokery – or so it said in the show rules listed in the catalogue, and Jerry always abided by the rules. He walked off down the path leading around the Crowley house to the garden at the back. He was closely followed by Johnny, who detested Crowley and was thoroughly enjoying the situation, with old Will, still dazed, bringing up the rear.

But he wasn't the only one dazed a minute later. He, Jerry and Johnny stood side by side gazing at the Crowley garden; they could scarce believe their eyes. For the garden which Crowley had boasted was the best kept vegetable garden in the district and the home of his gigantic marrows, was nothing less than a wilderness. It had the finest collection of weeds that any of them had ever seen and the whole place had obviously had nothing done to it in the two years Crowley had been living there. Talk about growing a prize winning marrow there – the very thought of it was ludicrous. Obviously he had only been able to get away with it because nobody had seen his secluded garden.

Jerry was the first to come to grips with the situation. "That settles it," he said quietly, and marched up to the back door and banged loudly; there was no answer.

"They're out, I think," said Johnny. "Don't suppose they'll be back before tonight."

"Reckon I'll have a surprise for them by then," said the show secretary, grimly. "I'm going to get as many of the committee as I can together. Then we'll soon sort out our friend Mr Crowley."

Jerry wasted no time. He had soon gathered together the nucleus of the committee and that night it was announced that

Arthur Crowley had been banned from the show for life.

The entire village celebrated. A deputation representing the Show Committee, the Whistler's Arms, the Royal British Legion, the Women's Institute and half a dozen other societies including even the Football and Cricket Clubs, went round to see Will and persuaded him to enter his marrow in the show. "Of course you were the winner last year really," they said. "We'll put it right in the records, don't you worry about that. Always suspected that Crowley never grew that marrow you know. Grown by his brother-in-law in the Midlands, you know. This one and last years. Champion marrow-grower of the Midlands apparently, his brother-in-law. And a commercial grower as well – he's got a Garden Centre and Nurseries. No wonder you didn't stand a chance Will. 'Course, they've got soil and climate with them up there, haven't they? And he's a professional grower."

Will agreed that was so, and also agreed to put his marrow in the show; so the deputation left, their mission completed. A couple of days afterwards the cup was back on Will's sideboard where it rightly belonged and the old man sat in his favourite armchair sucking at his pipe and gazing fondly at the handsome silver trophy – although there was a small niggle at the back of his mind when he recalled that Crowley had cheated him out of fifty pounds the previous year.

A couple of months later, Crowley and his family left the village for good. Transferred back to the Midlands or so he let it be known. As long as they didn't come back, nobody in the village cared a damn where they were going. The removal van passed Will's cottage with the Crowley family's lock, stock and barrel stacked aboard, and drove on towards the main road.

Will stood in his garden and watched the van disappear around the corner. And he couldn't help but feel that it was the best thing that had ever happened to him when Johnny Marker fell over in his lorry that afternoon and the crate had smashed. That little accident was responsible for Will Dobson feeling himself again. People respected him like they used to and talked to him like they had before, and he was a pillar in the community again, not an outcast, which was exactly what he had been since last year's show. And the cup was back on the sideboard. Yet he had won it with the smallest marrow he had ever entered in a show in his life. Still, that show was over and done with.

He picked up his turning fork and began to work in his garden. There was no time to waste – after all, there would be another show in ten months' time.